Is this secret formula for real?

The two boys watched the ground as if they expected something to jump out at them.

Nothing did.

"Forget about it," David said. "The worst that could happen is that the grass will grow really tall. Big deal. Let's just check out the plants and get back to the tent."

Luckily, the plant situation was under control.

"You see?" David said. "We've got nothing to worry about."

But David was wrong. He knew it the moment they headed back through the yard. Because long, green grass wasn't the only thing springing from the dirt.

DEADTIME STORIES™

Night of the Pet Zombies

A. G. Cascone

Troll

*For David and Jerry,
a couple of
"miracle workers"*

CHAPTER 1

David Brewster and his best friend, Eddie Deegan, sat on the edge of David's bed, watching in horror as Angelica Verdiana died a slow and terrible death.

Just days before, Angelica had been full of life, full of hope, full of promise. But now she was frail and weak. She was so dehydrated that the tiny purple veins under her skin were turning brown and collapsing. She couldn't even stand up anymore—not even with the help of the braces David and Eddie had made for her.

"She's not going to make it through the weekend, is she?" David said, feeling as if he were about to collapse too.

Eddie shook his head numbly. "I don't think she's even going to make it through the night."

"How could this happen?" David sighed. "She was doing great just a couple of days ago."

"Well, she's not doing great now." Eddie groaned. "I mean, look at her. She's so dry and crispy, I'm afraid to even touch her because her limbs will probably fall off."

David winced at the thought. If Angelica's limbs fell off, there would be no way they could bring her to school on Monday.

"Maybe we should give her a glass of water," David suggested. "Maybe that'll bring her around."

Eddie shot him a look. "It's a little late for that, don't you think? Now she's a goner."

"She is *not* a goner." David tried to convince himself that was true. "Look." He pointed to one of Angelica's limbs. "She's still got *some* color left."

But the color didn't last very long. As Angelica Verdiana lay dying in her own bed, a heartless scavenger was preparing to rip the last shred of life from her weak, pathetic body.

David gasped as he caught sight of the big black bug creeping across Angelica's bed. "Get away from her!" he screamed as he ran for his desk.

But before David could reach Angelica's flowerpot, the horrible creature attacked. With one quick bite, the bug snapped Angelica Verdiana's last healthy limb in two.

David could hear the disgusting creature chomping away on Angelica's last leaf.

There was no question about it now. Angelica Verdiana *was* a goner.

"I can't believe that big bug just killed Angelica," David said, glaring down at the creature.

"What the heck is that thing, anyway?" Eddie cringed.

"I don't know." David shrugged. "But I'm going to rip its hairy legs off for this!"

David was determined to exact revenge on the six-legged mutant who'd just destroyed the last remnants of his and Eddie's science project. But as he reached out to grab the bug, it quickly burrowed into Angelica's dirt.

"Dump the pot over," Eddie suggested. "Then bash its little head in."

"No way," David said. "If I turn the pot over, I'll mess up Angelica's roots."

"Who cares about Angelica's roots?" Eddie asked. "Without her leaves we don't have a science project. I mean, what are we going to do—stick her in the pot upside down and tell Mrs. Wolfe we grew a root plant from her vine seeds? I don't think she'll believe us."

It was Friday night, and David and Eddie were supposed to bring three thriving plants to science class Monday morning—a flower, a vine, and a fungus. Angelica Verdiana was the vine. The flower and fungus were already long dead. Their pathetic wilted bodies still sat in their pots on the desk next to Angelica.

"If we don't kill Angelica's roots, maybe she'll grow another shoot," David said.

"Yeah, right." Eddie sighed. "It took us three weeks just to get her to grow the first shoot. There's no way she's going to grow another one in two days." He threw himself

7

back on the bed, totally exasperated. "Why, why, *why* did you have to volunteer us to do these stupid plant seeds, anyway?" he complained for the ten millionth time.

"Because I thought it would be easy," David defended himself. "I thought we'd be able to buy a bunch of these plants already grown and ace this stupid science project without doing any work. How was I supposed to know that none of the plant stores carried them?"

The bug climbed out of the dirt and munched on Angelica's stem behind David's back.

"Yeah, well, maybe if you'd watered the plants when you were supposed to, we would have been able to ace this science project anyway," Eddie grumbled. "Last time I was over here, their flowerpots were as dry as the Gobi desert!"

"At least I didn't try to drown everybody!" David snapped. "If it weren't for you, Herbie would still be alive."

Herbie was short for some scientific name neither David nor Eddie could pronounce. He was their flower.

"I told you those little holes in the bottom of the pot were for draining water out, not sucking it in," David continued to rant. "But you wouldn't listen to me, would you? *Nooooooo.* You had to bring Herbie home and put him in your bathtub for three days. Now look at him. He's totally waterlogged!"

"Well, maybe if you'd put Angelica in *your* bathtub, last night, she wouldn't be all dry and crispy!" Eddie shot back.

"I did put her in the bathtub," David argued. "I even gave Ferd a massage, just like you said I should." Ferd was their fungus. "But all that did was give me an itchy rash that's driving me crazy."

The big bug turned its ugly head toward them, as if their bickering were disturbing its meal.

"Oh, no, pal!" David said, finally noticing the bug's presence. "No way you're going to eat Angelica Verdiana and get away with it." He reached for the pot. But Eddie pulled him away.

"Don't try to grab him when he's looking at you, stupid. He'll just bury himself in the dirt again. Wait until he looks away. Then we'll sneak up on him."

As soon as the bug went back to its dinner, David and Eddie crept toward the desk as silently as they could. But before they'd even reached their victim, an ominous figure appeared out of nowhere and began to creep up on *them*.

David felt the horrible presence at his back as its eerie shadow took shape on the wall. It looked like the Grim Reaper himself!

David was just about to spin around and scream when a bony, thin hand clamped over his mouth and hot, stinking breath hit his ear.

"You let them die!" The figure's voice was as ominous as its presence. "You let them all die, you naughty boy. That means you and your little friend die next!"

CHAPTER 2

Fear surged through David's body—until he saw the skull ring on the hand covering his mouth. He grabbed the hand and jerked it away hard. "Let go of me, Charley, you freak!"

Charley just laughed. "Why, of course, brother dear." She did her best late-show-vampire voice. "But I'll thank you to call me by my proper name, which is Charlotte."

"Yeah, right, Charley. That might happen," David responded.

David had always called his big sister Charley. And it had always been fine with her—until she became a teenager. That was when Charley decided that Charlotte sounded "positively medieval," which she liked. Her only regret was that she didn't live back in the Dark Ages, when blood, gore, and torture were the norm.

Charley had always been a little bit weird. But ever

since she'd turned thirteen, she'd gotten *really* freaky.

She always dressed in black—even at bedtime. And she always walked around acting intentionally morbid.

The more Charley irritated people, the more she liked it.

David's mother insisted that Charley's behavior had something to do with hormones and that she was just going through a stage that would probably pass quickly.

It wasn't passing quickly enough.

"Hey, Charley," Eddie said, noticing the black velvet lettering on the front of her Grim Reaper nightgown that read GLOOM. "Is that your favorite band, or just your favorite mood?"

Charley was always listening to heavy-metal bands like Gloom and Destructo—because everyone else hated them.

"It's definitely her favorite mood," David answered.

"Actually, it's both," Charley informed them. "But you two are going to be even gloomier than I am on Monday," she said, studying Angelica. "That's got to be the worst science project ever." She reached out to touch Angelica Verdiana's crunchy leaves. "The only part of plant life that you two morons will be able to demonstrate is plant death."

"Shut up, Charley!" David pulled his sister's hand from the vine.

"I only wish I could be there when you turn these plants in to Mrs. Wolfe. She's going to laugh in your faces. Mom and Dad, on the other hand, are not going to be laughing when you bring home another fat F."

Charley was right. David was already close to failing science. Three dead plants definitely weren't going to help.

Eddie was failing too—a detail Charley couldn't resist pointing out. "And given that you're just as stupid as my brother," she told Eddie, "you'll probably be shipped off to summer school too."

Terror flashed across Eddie's face as he looked at David.

"We're not going to summer school," David told Eddie, trying to sound sure of himself. "Because we're not going to fail."

"Oh, yes, you are," Charley said. "Unless you want to spend the rest of your life in the seventh grade, you're going to have to go to summer school." She laughed again, a normal, spontaneous laugh this time, rather than her practiced vampire laugh. "You guys are dead. So, so, *sooooooooo* dead!"

That did it! The boys chased Charley into her own room, with Charley laughing all the way.

Charley's room was painted black and decorated with posters of Gloom and Destructo and the sort of artwork normally seen on pinball machines. A solitary stuffed unicorn sitting in a forgotten corner of a bookshelf was the only indication of the earlier, sunnier Charley. An empty birdcage hung from the ceiling.

David saw a chance to get back at his big sister.

"Speaking of dead, Charley," David goaded, "your

stupid mynah bird has been dead for months now, and you still keep that cage. How lame is that?"

Charley grinned wickedly.

"What was that thing's name, anyway?" Eddie wanted to know.

"It was a *he*, not a *thing*," Charley answered indignantly. "And *his* name was Hitch."

"She named him after Alfred Hitchcock, remember?" David said.

"Oh, yeah," Eddie responded, "right after she saw that movie about birds pecking everyone's eyeballs out."

"The movie was called *The Birds*, you moron," Charley told him. "And Alfred Hitchcock was the most brilliant horror director of all time."

"Like we care," Eddie shot back.

"Yeah, well, Hitchcock the bird was *not* the most brilliant mynah of all time," David said, trying to crawl under Charley's skin. "The only thing he could say was, 'Hitch is a pretty bird.' My pet rock had more personality."

Eddie cracked up as Charley fumed.

"If I were you, I'd watch what I say around that cage," she warned David. "Hitch can still hear you. And trust me, he's anything but stupid. In fact, he's liable to peck *your* eyes out!"

David and Eddie exchanged looks.

"How the heck is a dead bird going to peck my eyes out?" Eddie asked.

Charley smirked. "Hitch's body may be dead," she said.

"But his spirit is alive and well and living in that cage. In fact, he's in there right now."

"He looks an awful lot like empty air," Eddie scoffed.

"Can't you see him, Eddie? He's glaring right at you," Charley insisted.

"He is not," Eddie snapped. "That cage is empty."

"You only think the cage is empty, because you have a little pea brain," Charley said. "People with little pea brains can't ever see the other side."

"The other side of what?" David wanted to know.

"The spirit world," Charley explained. "It exists all around us. But only those with superior intelligence are able to see it clearly."

"Yeah, right," David said.

"If you don't believe me, why don't you climb up on that chair and take a closer look at the bottom of the cage," Charley challenged.

"Why? So we can see empty air up close?" Eddie asked.

"No. Because Hitch still leaves droppings that even inferior pea brains can see. They're spirit droppings, so they glow in the dark."

"Get out of here." Eddie laughed. "*You're* full of droppings."

"What's the matter, Eddie?" Charley wouldn't let up. "Are you too afraid to look?"

"Yeah, that's it," Eddie said. "I'm afraid to look at spirit poop."

David snickered.

"You know what?" Charley went on. "Maybe it's better that you don't look—just in case Hitch decides to attack."

"Cut me a break," David said, climbing onto the chair. "That bird is not in that cage. And neither is his poop."

But David was in for the shock of his life as he peered into the cage. Not because he saw something supernatural, but because a voice as clear as day said, "Hitch is a pretty bird . . . who's about to peck your eyes out!"

CHAPTER 3

David nearly fell off the chair, catching his balance at the last second. It was then that he realized the voice he'd heard belonged to Charley.

"You jerk!" David shouted at his sister. "I could have broken my neck!"

Charley mocked him some more. "'Pretty bird.'" She imitated the mynah again. "'Hitch is a pretty bird.'" She doubled over with laughter. "You are so gullible," she told her brother. "*Sooooooo* gullible!"

"And you are going to be *sooooooo* grounded, young lady, if you don't stop pulling these stunts!" Another voice rang through the room.

It was Mrs. Brewster. She was standing in the doorway, looking as unamused as she sounded.

"It's their fault for being in my room!" Charley tried to defend herself.

"I don't want to hear it," Mrs. Brewster said firmly. "Your brother could have been hurt."

"Like I could get that lucky," Charley muttered under her breath.

"I heard that!" Mrs. Brewster barked. She stormed into the room to ream Charley but good. "I've had it with you and your morbidness and your crazy stories." Her voice rose along with her rage. "I mean it, Charley! I'm almost at the end of my rope!"

David grinned smugly as Charley turned even whiter than her vampire makeup.

Eddie, however, started to squirm. "Maybe we should get out of here before your mom's rope breaks," he whispered nervously to David.

David nodded. Eddie was right. When Mrs. Brewster went on a rampage, no one was safe. "Uh, Mom." He interrupted the fireworks cautiously. "Eddie and I are going downstairs to finish working on the signs for our science project, okay?"

"Just don't stay up too late," Mrs. Brewster ordered. "And don't get paint on anything. Otherwise your sister won't be the only one who's in big trouble. You got me?"

"We've already spread out newspaper," David said. "So you don't have to worry."

With that, the boys scooted out of the room and headed downstairs.

David and Eddie really *had* spread out newspaper in the family room to protect the furniture and carpeting from the paint they were using to make the signs for their disastrous science project. They'd even covered their sleeping bags, which were spread out as well.

Since Eddie was spending the weekend at David's, the two of them had been hoping to camp out in David's backyard. But thanks to the rainstorm raging outside, camping out in the family room was the best they could do.

"We don't really have to finish these signs tonight," David told Eddie. "I just said that to get out of that scene upstairs. We can work on these tomorrow."

"What for?" Eddie said. "There's no point in working on them at all since our plants are dead. I mean, what are we going to say? 'Here are a drowned flower, a crispy, dead vine, and a putrid, dead fungus'?"

"Who knows?" David replied. "Maybe Mrs. Wolfe will give us extra points for the artwork."

"Yeah, right." Eddie groaned. "Then we'll go from an F-minus to an F-plus. I say we just pack it all in and watch the zombie movie they've been advertising on that new cable station."

"You mean the Monster Channel?" David asked.

"Yeah. That's it," Eddie agreed. "The movie is called *The Zombies of Zanesville*."

"I think it already started," David said, reaching for the TV remote.

"Who cares?" Eddie shrugged. "It'll take my mind off going to summer school."

David turned on the TV and zapped over to the Monster Channel. Instead of the movie, a commercial was on—a commercial with a creepy-looking pitchman.

David and Eddie exchanged looks to confirm how weird the guy was.

He had no hair anywhere on his head, not even any eyebrows or eyelashes. His skin looked as if it hadn't seen daylight in months. And he had an intensity about him that was totally freaky.

"Yes, my friends," he said in a voice just as strange as his appearance. "I've discovered the miracle you've been searching for. Faster than you can imagine, more completely than you can believe, Miracle Life will bring even the most pathetic plants back to full bloom."

"Hey!" David blurted excitedly. "It's an ad for plant food or something. Is this lucky or what?"

"Shhh," Eddie hissed. "Let's see what it's supposed to do."

"Maybe you have twelve black thumbs," the pitchman continued. "There's no need to worry. Miracle Life can even bring *dead* plants back to glorious bloom. Yes, you heard right, friends. I said dead plants. D-E-A-D, dead!"

"How can that be?" Eddie wondered aloud.

"Shhhh!" This time it was David who hissed. "Just shut up and watch."

"Just shut up and watch," the pitchman echoed, as if *he'd* heard Eddie too. "You won't believe your eyes!"

David stayed glued to the screen as the Miracle Life guy sprinkled a grisly-looking concoction into a flowerpot containing a withered daisy. Its stem was nearly black, and its petals were dried to a crisp.

But the moment the Miracle Life touched its soil, the flower started to shiver—and change.

David and Eddie watched in amazement as the head of the daisy picked itself up from the dirt. A moment later, the stem straightened and color flowed into every part of the plant. Within seconds, the daisy was as alive and healthy-looking as it could be.

"That's got to be trick photography." Eddie refused to believe his own eyes. "Nothing could possibly do that for real."

"You just saw it!" David said, wanting to believe that Miracle Life was the answer to their problems. "They can't use trick photography on a commercial and say that it's real. There are laws against that kind of stuff. Maybe this weirdo really *has* discovered a miracle. Besides, what do we have to lose?"

"Twelve dollars and ninety-five cents," Eddie pointed out as the pitchman made it clear that Miracle Life was sold exclusively at one store. "And that store is downtown in the deserted old creepy section. Are you sure you want to go down there?"

"Yeah, I'm sure I want to go down there. You want to know why? Because I'm sure I don't want to fail science class! Anyway, downtown isn't really that bad. It'll be fine."

"It *will* be fine," the pitchman echoed again.

David couldn't believe his ears as he stared at the freak on the screen—who seemed to be staring back at him. But the stare-off lasted only a second before the

Miracle Life commercial faded out and *The Zombies of Zanesville* faded in—right in the middle of a climactic scene.

"That's weird," Eddie said. "How come a commercial just popped into the middle of the movie?"

"Who knows?" David responded. "And who cares? This movie looks pretty stupid anyway. I say we try to go to sleep so we can get up at six o'clock and head downtown to get this Miracle Life stuff before they sell out."

"You go to sleep," Eddie said. "I'm watching the movie."

David crawled into his sleeping bag and tried to get comfortable. But that was hard to do, because his itch was starting to act up again.

At least it seemed like an itch.

"I swear, I'm going to kill you for making me massage Ferd," he told Eddie, squirming in his sleeping bag.

"How was I supposed to know you'd get itchy?" Eddie argued. "Mrs. Wolfe didn't say anything about catching the heebie-jeebies from that thing."

But David *wasn't* itchy from the fungus. He realized that when his itch started doing something itches don't usually do. It started to crawl up his back—on six hairy legs.

One thing was certain. David was definitely not alone in his sleeping bag!

CHAPTER

4

"*Aaaaaaaagggggggghhhhh!*" David screamed as the itch crept up his neck, then climbed onto his cheek. It wasn't an itch at all. It was the same bug that had murdered Angelica. And it was headed straight for his eyeball!

"Get off me!" David cried, flicking the mega-bug across the room with his fingers.

"What's the matter with you?" Eddie yelled as David sprang from his sleeping bag.

"That big ugly bug was just in my bed!" David answered.

"You're kidding me, right?" Eddie said.

"No!" David snapped. "It's right over there." He pointed to the six-legged mutant, who was now creeping across the carpet.

"Aw, man." Eddie suddenly felt itchy too. "How the heck did it get down here?"

"I don't know," David said. "But it's not getting out alive, that's for sure." He headed toward the bug. "You are dead meat, buster," he told the creature.

"I'll get it," Eddie said. He tried to swat the bug with a magazine but missed.

"It's too fast." David reached for a can of spray paint as the bug ran for its life. "I'll get it with this. It's better than bug spray. Watch."

David approached the insect with the can of green paint he was planning to use for their Angelica Verdiana sign. "Take that!" he cried as he aimed for the bug's head.

But the little black monster scooted out of the way at the very last second, and the paint missed its mark.

Luckily, the newspaper was still covering the floor.

"You're not getting away that easily!" David insisted, trying to cut the bug off. He fired again. But the only thing he hit was Eddie's socks.

"Hey!" Eddie shouted. "These sweat socks are new!"

"Oh, stop whining," David said. "Who wants plain white socks anyway? They look cool painted green."

"Tell that to my mom," Eddie muttered as David turned his attention back to the bug.

The creepy creature scurried around the room, trying to find an opening to crawl through. Finally, it approached one of the corners of the room, and David's eyes lit up.

"Now I've got you!" David exclaimed. He aimed and fired again. This time, he hit the bug dead on. Its head turned the color of Eddie's socks, and it flipped onto its back with its front legs curled up.

"You killed him!" Eddie high-fived David. "You nailed that slimy little sucker!"

David picked up the bug by one of its hind legs, then shoved it in Eddie's face so he could see the bug up close and personal too.

"Ugggghhh." Eddie shoved David's hand away. "Thanks a lot, jerkface."

David laughed. "Come on," he said. "I've got an idea."

David headed out of the family room with the bug in his hands and Eddie at his heels.

"What are we going to do?" Eddie wanted to know as he followed David upstairs. "Drop it in Charley's bed?"

"Good idea," David said. "But way too risky. Everyone would know we did it, since its head is spray-painted green."

"Then what are we going to do with it?" Eddie asked.

"Ssshhh," David cautioned as they reached the landing upstairs. "We don't want to wake anyone up."

He tiptoed down the hall into his room and dropped the bug into the flowerpot grave of Angelica Verdiana.

"What are you doing that for?" Eddie asked.

"For fertilizer," David answered. "In case that Miracle Life stuff turns out to be a scam."

"You dragged me all the way upstairs to do that?" Eddie groaned.

David nodded. "Who knows? Maybe it'll work."

"And maybe my mom will think my socks are cool, too," Eddie grumbled as he headed for the door. "I'm going back downstairs to finish watching the movie."

David followed, only to hear the TV announcer say, "You just saw *The Zombies of Zanesville* on the Monster Channel. We hope you enjoyed it."

"Hardly," Eddie complained.

"Stay tuned for a preview of the midnight madness coming your way on the Monster Channel this month, absolutely commercial-free."

David shot Eddie a look as a chill crept up his spine.

If the Monster Channel was commercial-free, where did the commercial for Miracle Life come from?

CHAPTER

5

"How much do you want to bet that Miracle Life commercial was just a joke?" Eddie said as he and David cautiously made their way through the deserted streets in the bad part of town.

It was seven-thirty the next morning, but the city seemed dark and foreboding.

"What do you mean?" David asked, nervously scanning the boarded-up buildings.

"I mean there probably is no Miracle Life store," Eddie said. "You heard that announcer. The Monster Channel is supposed to be commercial-free. That 'commercial' was just a gag."

"No way," David said. "It wasn't even funny."

"Yeah, well, maybe *they* thought it was funny," Eddie went on. "I mean, look at this street. It's totally deserted."

"The commercial wasn't a gag," David insisted. "Miracle Life has to exist."

"Not on this street, it doesn't," Eddie said.

"Maybe we're on the wrong block," David suggested. He was just about to turn back the way they came when something in the distance caught his eye.

"Look!" David exclaimed. "There it is!" He pointed to the flashing red sign up ahead. Then he grabbed Eddie's arm and picked up his pace.

"How do you know that's the right place?" Eddie asked as David dragged him down the street.

"Because it's the only store on this block that's open, you idiot," David answered. "And the sign says 'Stop Here For a Miracle.' What else could it be?"

As David reached the door of the shop, Eddie pulled back. "This place doesn't look open to me," he said nervously.

The windows of the shop were all boarded up, and the door looked as if it was about to fall from its hinges.

"Let's go inside," David said, shaking off his own fear. "I'll bet somebody's in there."

"That's what I'm afraid of." Eddie gulped.

David pushed open the creaking wood door. Then he and Eddie stepped inside a flower shop.

The problem was, it looked as though it hadn't been open in years.

Every inch of the store was covered with dust, including the floor. And while dozens of plants occupied the shelves, they were all black and crispy—because they were all deader than dead.

David's heart sank.

"I told you that commercial was a gag," Eddie said, looking around the dark, musty shop. "This place is deserted."

"At this hour, what do you expect?" An unearthly voice floated from the back of the store.

David gasped, while Eddie let out a full-blown scream.

A moment later, the owner of the voice crept out of the shadows. "I didn't mean to startle you." The man looked deader than dead himself. "But I wasn't planning on customers this early."

For a moment, David thought he recognized the guy from *The Zombies of Zanesville*, until he remembered. "Holy smokes!" he said, staring at the hairless head and crumpled black tuxedo. "It's you!"

"Of course it's me," the bald weirdo replied. "Were you expecting someone else?"

"No," David said. "I just wasn't expecting *you*."

"Expecting who?" Eddie yelped. "Who is this guy?"

"It's the guy from the Miracle Life commercial," David told him.

"Hey!" Eddie exclaimed. "You're right! It *is* him!"

"I see my celebrity precedes me," the salesman said in slow, measured tones. "Allow me to introduce myself. My name is Frederick von Mortmeister. And I *was* expecting *you*—just not quite this early." He extended his ash-white hand to David.

To be polite, David extended his hand as well.

The moment Mortmeister wrapped his fingers around David's, David shuddered.

28

Mortmeister's grip wasn't just cold, it was frigid. Even worse, his flesh seemed downright loose, as though it might fall off the bone at any second.

David tried to pull away, but Mortmeister tightened his grip.

"Cold hands, warm heart," he said. Then he smiled like the Cheshire cat, exposing a mouthful of rotting gray teeth.

David forced a smile in return, but Eddie turned his head, cringing.

Finally, Mortmeister released his grip. Then he bit four of his fingernails down to the quick and spit them onto the floor.

David shot Eddie a look. This guy was even grosser in person than he was in the commercial.

"So what can I do you for?" Mortmeister asked. "Don't tell me," he went on before the boys had a chance to speak. "You want a miracle."

David nodded.

"It's what everybody wants," Mortmeister said. "Yes, my friend, everyone wants Miracle Life." He reached into the pocket of his tuxedo and pulled out a handful of something that looked like meatloaf vomit. Then he chuckled the same way Charley did when she was imitating the undead and began plopping the stuff into various flowerpots.

David watched in amazement as the plants sprang back to life!

"So here's the miracle," Mortmeister whispered over

his shoulder as he continued to rejuvenate every plant in the store. "For the dead, there is life. And for the living, only death. Sad for some," he said, grinning his rotten-toothed smile at David again. "But thrilling for others."

"What's that supposed to mean?" Eddie asked, sounding as creeped-out as David felt.

"You'll find out soon enough," Mortmeister assured them. "But not until you get what you came for." He headed toward the back of the store.

It was then that David noticed the strange blotch on the back of Mortmeister's neck. It looked as if someone had bitten out a chunk of his flesh. But Mortmeister pulled up his collar so quickly, David couldn't be sure.

"This guy is too freaky for words," Eddie said. "Maybe we should just get out of here while he's not looking."

"No way," David told him. "I'm not leaving until we get that Miracle Life. Look what it did to these plants. If our plants end up looking half as good as these, we're definitely going to get an A!"

Eddie couldn't argue with that. "Let's get out of here as soon as we can, okay?"

David nodded. He had no desire to spend a lot of time with Mortmeister either.

Luckily, the creepy salesman reappeared a few moments later with a plastic sack about the size of a big potato chip bag. Across the top of the sack, written in black, squiggly letters, were the words "Miracle Life."

It looked like the same kind of lettering that was splattered across Charley's Destructo T-shirts.

"This will be more than enough for several lifetimes," Mortmeister assured them as he handed the sack to David. Then he absentmindedly bit off his thumbnail and spit it between Eddie's eyes.

"Aw, man!" Eddie cried, wiping frantically at his face. "That's disgusting!"

"Sorry, my friend," Mortmeister apologized. "Let me try to make it up to you." He thought for a second, rubbing the skin on his forehead. Unfortunately, he rubbed a big patch of skin right off.

David winced at the sight.

"Too much exposure to the sun," Mortmeister explained, balling the rubbed-off skin between two fingers. "I'll have to get some skin cream."

David forced another smile.

"I'll tell you what," Mortmeister finally said. "I'll give you the Miracle Life for half price. Does that seem fair?"

"It sure does." David jumped on the offer.

"Yes," Mortmeister said. "Six dollars and forty-eight cents seems like a very fair price for a miracle."

As David dug into his pocket for the money, he noticed something strange moving on the floor by his feet.

At first David thought it was tiny, winged bugs. Then he blinked hard and realized that the objects scooting past him were much more disgusting than bugs.

Mortmeister's fingernail scraps were alive! They were creeping across the floor all by themselves.

CHAPTER 6

"That's impossible," Eddie said, shaking his head. "No way Mortmeister's fingernails were walking."

"I'm telling you," David insisted as he switched the bag of Miracle Life from his right shoulder to his left. "They were tiptoeing across the floor."

Eddie just laughed.

"What's so funny?" David asked.

"Tiptoeing fingernails?" Eddie said. "Do you know how ridiculous that sounds?"

David laughed too, despite the fact that he was still convinced it was true. He *had* seen tiptoeing fingernails, even though there was no way he was going to get Eddie to believe it. He'd been trying to convince him all the way home.

"You didn't even see the big thumbnail?" David gave it one last shot as they headed up his driveway.

"Only when it hit me in the face," Eddie said. "You probably just saw a pack of termites. That place had to be infested."

David sighed, allowing the subject to drop. There was another subject he needed to turn his attention to now— their science project.

"Mom, we're home!" David called out as he and Eddie stepped through the front door.

"Did you get the plant food you were looking for?" Mrs. Brewster asked from the kitchen.

"Yeah," David shouted back. "We got it at Hinkle's Hardware Store, just like I said we would. And the store *was* open when we got there."

"You told your mom we went to Hinkle's?" Eddie mouthed to David.

"I had to," David whispered back. "If I told her we were going downtown at the crack of dawn, she never would have let us go."

"Good point," Eddie acknowledged.

"Just make sure you stick to the Hinkle's story, okay?" David warned.

"Don't worry," Eddie assured him. "I will."

"Are you boys hungry?" Mrs. Brewster called.

"No, Mom," David answered. "We ate some cereal before we left. If you need us, we'll be upstairs working on our project."

As soon as David and Eddie hit David's room, David plopped down on his bed and tore open the bag of Miracle Life. "I say we save Angelica first."

"Works for me," Eddie responded as David peered into the bag. "How's it look?"

"The same way it looked at Mortmeister's." David grimaced.

"Like puke?" Eddie asked.

David nodded. "Stick your hand in there and grab some," he said.

"*You* stick your hand in there and grab some," Eddie shot back. "I'm not touching that stuff."

David didn't want to touch it either, but he wasn't about to admit that to Eddie. "It's just some kind of fast-acting fertilizer," he said. "It's not going to hurt you."

"It's not going to hurt you either," Eddie argued. "So you pick it up."

"Fine," David huffed. "I will."

The moment he reached into the bag, he crinkled his nose. Picking up Miracle Life really did feel like picking up a handful of chunky brown vomit.

"Let me see it," Eddie said as David pulled his hand from the bag. "Gross. This stuff looks even worse than puke."

David couldn't possibly imagine anything worse-looking than puke—until Eddie spelled it out.

"It looks like chopped-up body parts, all clumped together like rotten hamburger meat, doesn't it?"

David's stomach lurched at the thought.

"And check this out," Eddie continued, pointing to a bunch of white flecks sticking out of the clump. "These look like toenail clippings!"

Now David wanted to get the Miracle Life out of his hand and into Angelica's pot as quickly as he could. "Get out of my way," he said, racing for the desk.

He plopped the gunk on top of Angelica's soil, covering the dead bug too. Then he wiped his hand on his shorts as Angelica's soil started to suck . . .

And slurp . . .

And bubble . . .

And belch.

"Whoa," Eddie yelled. "Looks like Angelica is really eating that stuff up!"

"For real," David agreed. "Even Mortmeister's plants weren't making that noise."

Just then, Angelica started to shiver and change, just like the daisy they'd seen on TV.

Her hunched-over spine stood up straight, and every collapsed vein in her body turned from brown to violet.

Her tendrils even grabbed at the braces David and Eddie had made for her.

But Angelica didn't need the braces for long. Within seconds, her leaves grew as strong and as firm as her stem. She even grew twelve new shoots!

"Holy smoke!" Eddie shouted. "This is too cool!"

"This is better than cool," David said. "This is definitely an A-plus! Get some Miracle Life for Herbie."

Eddie was so excited about reviving their flower, he didn't even flinch as he spread on the Miracle Life.

A few moments later, Herbie looked more like Hercules.

"Check out Ferd," David said, feeding the fungus.

"Don't touch him," Eddie warned. "Otherwise you'll be itching again."

David stepped back as the fungus reached forward.

"How the heck does this stuff work?" Eddie was in awe of their accomplishments.

"Who knows?" David said. "All that matters is that it *does* work. And we're not going to summer school!"

"Yes!" Eddie gave David a high-five. "Too bad we can't find some kind of Miracle Life for history class."

"For real." David laughed. "But at least we'll ace science this semester!"

"I can't believe it," Eddie said. "All we've got to do now is finish those stupid signs."

"Yeah. But we don't have to finish them today," David decided. "We've got all day tomorrow. I say we grab our skates and hit the park. It's beautiful out."

"Good idea!" Eddie agreed.

"I bet the ground will be dry enough for us to camp out tonight too," David added excitedly as he grabbed their in-line skates from his closet. "Maybe my mom will even barbecue for us."

"Cool," Eddie said. "I could definitely go for that."

Finally, it was turning into a worry-free weekend.

In fact, David and Eddie had such a good time in the park that Mrs. Brewster and Charley were already preparing the cook-out by the time they got back.

"Sorry we're late, Mom," David apologized. "We lost track of time."

"It's okay, boys," Mrs. Brewster said. "You can help with

the cleanup after dinner. Now why don't you go clean *yourselves* up before we're ready to eat?"

"You'd better use some serious disinfectant," Charley told David and Eddie. "Because you both smell like dung."

"We do not," David hissed.

"Yes, you do," Charley said. "And you look like dung too."

"Charlotte!" their mother snapped. "That's enough."

"I'm just telling the truth, Mother."

Mrs. Brewster crinkled her nose. "Something really does smell bad in here, doesn't it?"

Charley nodded smugly.

"It's not me," David said, turning on Eddie. "He's the one who didn't take a shower this morning."

"Hey!" Eddie protested. "You're just as ripe as I am!"

Mrs. Brewster chuckled. "Calm down, you two," she said. "There's certainly a funny smell in here, but it's not coming from you boys."

"Then where is it coming from?" Charley wanted to know.

"From you," David said. "It's probably that Eau de Death perfume you wear."

"Drop dead, you toad," Charley snarled.

"It's not coming from any of you." Mrs. Brewster sniffed the air. "I think it's coming from the foyer." She headed out of the kitchen into the hallway with David, Eddie, and Charley right at her heels.

While the smell in the foyer was foul, and much

stronger than the odor in the kitchen, it was clear that the foyer wasn't the source of the problem.

"Where the heck is this coming from?" Mrs. Brewster wondered as she followed her nose up the stairs with the kids right behind her.

But they'd only made it halfway up when something stopped them dead in their tracks.

CHAPTER 7

Ka-boom!

The sound that exploded from behind David's bedroom door was deafening. Not only did it stop everyone's feet, it stopped David's heart.

"What the heck was that?" Mrs. Brewster asked.

"I don't know," David answered. He nervously followed his mother the rest of the way upstairs, with Eddie and Charley in tow.

"It sounded like something big fell over," Eddie said as they rushed down the hall.

Mrs. Brewster threw open the door to David's room. Then she let out a gasp and covered her nose.

"What's going on?" David said as the stench nearly made him gag.

Before Mrs. Brewster could answer, David pushed his way past her and saw for himself. "Holy smoke!" he cried.

"Angelica Verdiana knocked the shelf off the wall!"

Angelica Verdiana had grown so tall and so strong that she'd pushed the shelf above her head right off its brackets. Video-game cartridges and schoolbooks lay in a heap on the floor.

Eddie's jaw dropped. "She's ten times the size she was this morning!"

"Who's Angelica?" Mrs. Brewster asked, confused.

"Angelica Verdiana," David said, pointing to the overgrown plant. "She's the vine we grew for our science project."

"Wasn't she dead last night?" Charley asked, covering her nose.

"Yeah," Eddie answered. "But the plant food we got downtown this morning gave her new life."

Mrs. Brewster frowned suspiciously.

"He means downtown at Hinkle's," David explained, elbowing Eddie.

"Yeah." Eddie caught on. "I mean downtown at Hinkle's," he told Mrs. Brewster.

"Sure you do," Charley sneered.

"Anyway," Eddie continued as David glared at Charley, "the plant food turned Angelica into the King Kong of the plant world, because that shelf must weigh a ton! No way she pushed it right off the wall!"

"No way, indeed," Mrs. Brewster scoffed as she pointed to the wall. "One of the pegs snapped off, and the shelf just gave way. Thank goodness there was nothing breakable on it."

"Yeah, well, Angelica smells like rotten eggs," Charley said, covering her mouth and nose with the neck of her Destructo T-shirt. "And your flower smells like rotten feet. Not to mention that it's starting to look pretty hairy."

David and Eddie gave Herbie the once-over, then exchanged worried glances. Herbie *was* getting hairy.

"And you might want to look at this, Mother," Charley said, pointing to Ferd. "Their fungus is oozing all over the desk."

Mrs. Brewster shrieked. Ferd was dripping black gunk over the edge of the desk and onto the floor. "What's the matter with you boys?" she scolded. "Why would you keep such filthy, stinking plants in the house?"

"They weren't filthy and stinking before we fed them," David said. "Honest, Mom."

Mrs. Brewster rolled her eyes. "They couldn't possibly have just gotten filthy and stinky, David. They're stinking up my whole house!"

"Busted," Charley said, sounding pleased.

"The Miracle Life did this, Mom," David tried to convince her.

"I don't care what did it, David. Just take these plants outside where they belong. Then clean up this mess while I finish getting dinner ready," she ordered. "Leave the shelf. Your father will fix it later."

David knew there was no point in arguing with his mom. He and Eddie did as they were told.

They moved the plants outside, next to the fence that separated the Brewsters' house from the "Evil Ellises"—the Brewsters' next-door neighbors.

"Geez, oh, man," Eddie said when they were done. "They smell pretty stinky out here too."

"Good," David said. "Maybe they'll stink up the Ellises' yard."

"Why do you want to stink up their yard?" Eddie asked.

"Because we hate them," David explained. "They're the ones who called the cops on us last Fourth of July because my dad played the stereo outside, remember?"

"Oh, yeah."

"And their stupid dog is always ripping up our garbage," David continued, "and their cat is always sneaking over here to kill the squirrels in our yard."

"That's disgusting," Eddie groaned.

"So are the Ellises. Come on," David said, heading back toward the house. "Let's go clean up my room before Mom has a bird."

"Why do you think the plants got so smelly?" Eddie asked as he followed David to the house.

"Who knows?" David shrugged. "Maybe they're supposed to get smelly."

"Mrs. Wolfe didn't say they were going to stink," Eddie pointed out.

"She didn't say that Ferd was going to make me itchy either," David reminded him.

"You've got a point," Eddie acknowledged.

"All I know is that they're bigger than any plants I've ever seen," David said. "And that's what we want."

"You think they'll be okay out here until Monday?" Eddie asked.

"They'll probably do even better out here than inside," David answered, opening the sliding glass door that led into the kitchen.

"We'll be ready to eat in about twenty minutes," Mrs. Brewster told them as they passed through. "So get a move on. And make sure you wash your hands."

"Okay, Mom." David and Eddie headed up to David's room to clean up the mess.

But as they retrieved the video-game cartridges, David got sidetracked.

"Aw, man," David said, picking up The Undead Gladiator Ninjas of Doom. "I haven't played this one in ages. It's too cool."

"You want to try it?" Eddie asked.

"Yeah," David said. "We can clean up the rest of this stuff after dinner." He headed to his bookshelf to pop the tape into his game player and turn on the TV. But the cartridge wouldn't go in all the way. "Something's jamming this thing," he told Eddie.

"Stick your hand in there," Eddie said. "Maybe there's another cartridge inside."

"If there was another cartridge in there, this one wouldn't go in at all," David argued. But he stuck his hand in the slot just the same.

A moment later, he wished he hadn't.

Something stinky and hairy attacked his fingertips! And it wasn't another game cartridge.

CHAPTER 8

David pulled his hand out of the slot in panic. "Something just bit me!" he told Eddie, examining his fingers.

"What do you mean, something bit you?" Eddie asked. "Let me see."

David held out his hand, but there wasn't a scratch to be seen.

"Nothing bit you," Eddie scoffed.

"Something *tried* to bite me," David insisted. "I'm telling you, there's something in that machine."

"Like what?" Eddie asked.

"I don't know," David said. "But it had fangs!"

Suddenly, a hideous green face with antennae popped out of the opening.

"Oh, man!" David cried as the rest of the creature slid out of the slot, then leaped to the floor. "It's the bug!"

"It can't be!" Eddie said as the bug tore across the room and disappeared behind the dresser. "You killed that sucker last night!"

"Yeah, well, he's not dead now!" David slowly approached the chest of drawers.

"This has to be a different bug," Eddie insisted as David cautiously peered behind the dresser.

"There's no way it's a different bug," David said. "It has a green head! It's the same stupid bug from last night."

"That's impossible." Eddie refused to believe it. "Besides, it didn't even look like the same bug. This one was much bigger than the one you killed."

"Well, maybe it grew," David suggested.

"You're nuts," Eddie said. "Dead things don't grow! And they don't come back to life either!"

"You know what?" David grumbled. "Charley's right. You *do* have a pea brain, with the memory of a gnat! Don't you remember what happened to our dead plants?" He didn't wait for an answer. "They sprang back to life just like that!" He snapped his fingers. "And that bug was in Angelica's pot when we fed her, remember?"

"What are you saying?" Eddie asked. "That Miracle Life brought the bug back too?"

"That's exactly what I'm saying," David answered.

"No way!" Eddie shook his head adamantly. "It just couldn't happen. Plants and bugs are two different things, you dork. There's no way—"

"Shut up!" David said suddenly. "There it is!" He pointed to the wall above the bookcase.

Luckily, the bug stood still long enough for Eddie to get a good look at it.

He couldn't deny what he saw.

David was right on all counts. The bug had come back to life. And it was mutating before their very eyes.

CHAPTER 9

David watched in horror as the bug doubled in size. In less than a heartbeat, the slimy creature went from the size of a beetle to the size of a giant palmetto bug. Its six legs sprouted wiry black hair. So did its back and its spray-painted head.

But it was the sight of the globby black gook oozing out of the bug's mouth that made David gag.

Eddie gulped. "What the heck is happening to that thing?"

"I don't know." David cringed. "But it's getting all hairy like Herb. And it's oozing black gunk like Ferd!"

"Uh-oh." Eddie gasped. "What if it grows as big as Angelica?"

"Don't even say that!" David shrieked.

"I'm serious. What if it grows even bigger than us?

And what if it tries to get revenge on us for killing it in the first place?"

Just then, Mrs. Brewster called out from the bottom of the stairs.

She startled David so badly, he nearly hit the ceiling.

Eddie let out a bloodcurdling scream.

That startled the bug, which headed for cover.

"What's the matter with you?" David said. "You just scared the bug! Now we might not be able to find it again!"

"Yeah, well, your mother scared me!" Eddie defended himself.

"She was only calling us for dinner, you dork."

"You're the one who jumped," Eddie said.

"What's wrong?" Mrs. Brewster suddenly appeared in the doorway, with Mr. Brewster right behind her.

"What's all the screaming about?" he asked, alarmed.

"Nothing, Dad," David lied.

"Nothing?" Mrs. Brewster repeated incredulously. "That was some scream for nothing."

"What's the matter, Eddie?" Mr. Brewster tried again. "You look like you've just seen a ghost."

"Actually, it was more like a zombie," Eddie mumbled.

Mr. and Mrs. Brewster exchanged looks. Then Mr. Brewster cracked a smile. "You saw a zombie?" he asked.

Eddie nodded.

"Where?"

Eddie shrugged. "I think it's behind the dresser again."

Mr. Brewster peered behind the chest of drawers.

"That's funny," he said. "I don't see a zombie back here."

"It's a bug zombie, Dad." David knew he had no choice but to explain. "It's a big, black, hairy bug zombie with a green painted head."

Mr. Brewster shook his head. "Nope. I don't see that either, Dave." He chuckled.

"It's not funny, Dad," David said. "There really *is* a bug zombie in here."

"Terrific." Mrs. Brewster sighed. "Now we've got three Charleys in the house."

"No, Mom," David protested. "We're not making it up. You know that plant food we got this morning, downtown—"

"At Hinkle's," Eddie blurted out quickly, elbowing David this time.

"Well, not only did it bring our plants back to life, but it brought a dead bug back to life too," David continued. "We killed it last night and put it in Angelica's flowerpot. It was in there this morning when we fed her the Miracle Life. But we just saw it walking across the wall!"

"It must have been a different bug, Dave," Mr. Brewster said, sounding a little more sympathetic.

"No, Dad, it wasn't," David insisted. "Because this bug's head was spray-painted green too!"

Mr. and Mrs. Brewster looked confused.

"That's how we killed the thing," Eddie explained. "We sprayed it with paint."

Mrs. Brewster gave David a disapproving look.

"Don't worry, Mom. We didn't hit anything but the bug."

"And my socks," Eddie added.

This time David nudged him.

"To tell you the truth," Mrs. Brewster said, "between the garbage under that bed and those filthy, stinking plants, I wouldn't be surprised if you had an army of green-headed bugs crawling around this room."

"You're missing the point, Mom," David said. "We're trying to tell you that the bug we just saw was the same bug we killed last night!"

"For real, Mrs. Brewster." Eddie backed him up. "I'm telling you, it's like *Dead Bug Walking* in here."

"Look," Mr. Brewster said. "If the bug you saw really was the same bug, maybe you guys only stunned it with the spray paint last night. Maybe it wasn't really dead. Maybe it was just in a coma."

Mrs. Brewster chuckled.

"Could that really happen?" Eddie asked.

"I don't see why not," Mr. Brewster said. "It happens to people. Why can't it happen to bugs?"

"Oh, man." Eddie heaved a sigh of relief. "I bet your dad is right," he told David. "I mean, imagine if you'd gotten blasted with a huge cloud of poisonous green chemicals. You'd probably pass out too. And when you woke up, you'd probably mutate, just like it did."

"Cut me a break," David said. "That bug wasn't in a coma, and you know it. It was dead! At least until this morning."

"That's enough," Mrs. Brewster admonished. "You know very well that just can't be so, David. Now why don't you go wash your hands for dinner so we can get this barbecue started sometime before midnight."

"But, Mom—" David protested, but his father cut him off.

"But, Mom, nothing," he said. "You heard your mother. Go wash up." He scooted the boys through the door and pointed toward the bathroom.

"But, Dad—" David started again, but his father shook his head.

"I don't want any bug talk at dinner either," Mr. Brewster added as he and Mrs. Brewster headed back downstairs.

"Uggggghh!" David groaned. "How come parents never believe a word you say?"

"I believe you, brother dear." Charley suddenly appeared from her room, wearing a black dress. "In fact, I think you should bring your plant food to the cemetery tonight and raise Aunt Louise from the dead. I've always wanted to meet her. And this would be way better than a seance."

"Get out of my way, Morticia," David snapped as he shoved past Charley, with Eddie in tow.

"Your sister's sick in the head," Eddie said.

"Tell me about it," David agreed as they headed into the bathroom. "But she gave me an idea."

"Oh, no. No way we're bringing that plant food out to the cemetery," Eddie told David.

David grinned devilishly. "Oh, yes, we are," he said. "Just not to the cemetery Aunt Louise is buried in."

CHAPTER 10

"I'm not sure this is such a good idea," Eddie whispered as he and David snuck away from the picnic table and headed over to the cemetery by the side of David's house.

"Sure it is," David said, staring down at the tombstones.

Actually, the tombstones were rocks. And the cemetery belonged to David and Charley's dear departed pets.

"I don't know." Eddie sounded uneasy. "This whole thing seems pretty creepy to me."

"Look," David insisted. "All we've got to do is bring one dead pet back to life, and everyone will believe us about the bug. Not to mention the fact that I'd love to get Bullet and Dershowitz back."

Bullet was David's turtle. Dershowitz was a snake.

"I thought you said we were going to bring *one* dead pet back to life," Eddie grumbled.

"Two," David said sheepishly.

"If we're going to bring back dead pets, why don't we go over to the *real* cemetery and bring back your Aunt Louise? Then your mom will really believe us."

"No, she won't," David disagreed. "Aunt Louise was like a great-great-*great* aunt, so nobody ever met her. My mom doesn't even know what she looks like. Besides, there's no way Miracle Life would work on people."

"Then what makes you think it's going to work on animals?" Eddie asked. "I mean, maybe it just works on plants and bugs."

"That's why we're going to wait until later to try it," David said. "That way, if it doesn't work, nobody will be laughing in our faces."

"Hey!" Mr. Brewster came up behind them. "I thought you guys were supposed to be helping your mom clear off the table."

"We are, Dad," David said, spinning around. "I just wanted to show Eddie where . . . uh . . . Charley buried Hitch."

"Why?" his dad asked.

Help! David thought as he shot Eddie a look. *Think of something, will you?*

"Because Charley told me he was still alive," Eddie said, coloring the truth just a bit.

"Yeah," David backed him up. "Yesterday she tried to tell us that Hitch was still in his cage."

Mr. Brewster shook his head. "She's trying to kill us all, isn't she?" Mr. Brewster always said that when Charley's behavior exasperated him.

53

David nodded.

"Well, now that you've seen the bird's grave," Mr. Brewster continued, "why don't you go see all the garbage your mom is waiting for you to put out?"

"No problem, Dad," David said. "We'll take care of it real fast so we can start pitching our tent."

"I don't know about that, David," Mr. Brewster said. "The ground's still kind of soggy for camping."

"Yeah, but Mom said we could lay plastic down under our sleeping bags. Come on, Dad," David begged. "Eddie and I are dying to sleep out. And it's not like the ground is soaked."

Mr. Brewster finally gave in. "You guys win. A camp-out it is. I'll even help you pitch your tent."

David winced at the suggestion. His dad really enjoyed doing outdoorsy stuff, but he wasn't very good at it. And it usually took him forever to put up a tent because he was a perfectionist. "You don't have to do that, Dad," David said. "Eddie and I can handle it."

"I know you can handle it, Dave." Mr. Brewster smiled. "But I'd really *like* to help."

David forced a smile back. "Great," he lied.

Two hours later, Mr. Brewster was *still* helping.

"I told you the ground wasn't soggy," David said as his dad struggled to drive yet another spike into the lawn.

"The ground *is* soggy, Dave," Mr. Brewster replied. "I just keep hitting a root or something."

"So leave that one out," David suggested, eager to get the show on the road.

His father frowned. "How many times do I have to tell you, if you're going to do something, do it right or don't do it at all." He swung the hammer again.

And again . . .

And again.

"Maybe we should just move the tent over a few inches," he finally decided.

"Not for real!" David groaned.

"It'll only take me a few minutes, Dave," Mr. Brewster insisted. "Why don't you guys get all your stuff from the house? By the time you're back out again, your accommodations will be ready."

"Yeah, right," David mumbled under his breath as he and Eddie walked away. "It took him forty minutes just to hammer in the first three spikes. At this rate, our 'accommodations' won't be ready until tomorrow."

Eddie laughed. "I guess we'll have to forget about the pet cemetery stuff," he said.

"Why?" David asked.

"Because it's already getting dark."

"What difference does that make?" David wanted to know.

"A lot," Eddie answered. "No way I'm doing this in the dark."

"We've got a flashlight, you idiot," David said. "We'll be able to see things just fine."

By the time David and Eddie finished rounding up the gear inside the house, including munchies and Miracle Life, Mr. Brewster really was almost finished.

55

"You see," he said as they headed across the lawn. "I told you I'd be done in a jiff. I've just got two more spikes to drive in, then it's all yours."

"Terrific, Dad. I'm impressed." Still, David knew that two more spikes meant at least twenty more minutes. He dropped off the gear and decided to put the time to good use. "Let's go check on our plants," he told Eddie.

"Why?" Eddie asked.

"Because that big ugly bug is still missing," David whispered as he pulled Eddie aside. "And the only way to know what's happening to the bug is to find out what's happening to our plants. If they're still growing, so is the bug. And if that's the case, I've got to get my mom to call the exterminator."

"What happens if they *are* still growing? I mean, what if we bring back your pets and they start to grow too?"

"Then we'll just bring back Bullet," David answered. "What's the big deal about an overgrown turtle?"

"I guess," Eddie said. "But if he gets really big, you'll have to sell him to Sea World."

"Will you just shut up and come look at these plants!" David snapped. He and Eddie headed to the back of the yard with the Miracle Life and the flashlight in hand.

"Why are you bringing the Miracle Life?" Eddie asked.

"In case the plants are dead again," David said. "That's a possibility too. Who knows how long this stuff lasts?"

"Just don't drop it," Eddie warned.

"Like I'd really do that," David scoffed—right before he tripped over a tree root.

Not only did David go flying, so did the Miracle Life.

"Oh, man!" Eddie cried as the chunky brown gunk hit the dirt. "Look what you did!" He turned on the flashlight and pointed it at the mound of Miracle Life.

"Scoop it back up," David gasped.

"I can't," Eddie informed him. "Your yard is sucking at it!"

David heard the slurping sound and quickly rolled to his feet.

The two boys watched the ground as if they expected something to jump out at them.

Nothing did.

"Forget about it," David said. "The worst that could happen is that the grass will grow really tall. Big deal. Let's just check out the plants and get back to the tent."

Luckily, the plant situation was under control. Angelica, Herbie, and Ferd were no bigger than they had been hours before. And while they were all stinking up a storm, they were still alive.

"You see?" David said. "We've got nothing to worry about."

But David was wrong. He knew it the moment they headed back through the yard—because long green grass wasn't the only thing springing from the dirt.

CHAPTER 11

It wasn't the sight of the two-foot-tall blades of grass shooting up from the earth that stopped David in his tracks. It was the sight of the maggots . . .

And worms . . .

And the fat, juicy slugs.

Unfortunately, the worms had already slimed the bottom of David's sneakers, so his feet slid out from under him.

Eddie slipped too—right on top of a pile of slugs.

"Aaaaaaagggggghhhhhhhh!" the two of them wailed simultaneously.

"Somebody help me!" Eddie cried. "I'm getting eaten by zombie slugs!"

"Shut up!" David screamed back, struggling to escape the slugfest himself. "I don't want my dad to see this!"

"Are you nuts?" Eddie yelped. "We're covered in zombie

slugs!" He swiped at the bugs as he rose to his feet. "They're in my hair! THEY'RE IN MY HAIR!"

"Calm down!" David said, trying to stay calm himself. "They're not in your hair. And they're not zombie slugs. They're just regular slugs."

"We're standing in the same spot you dropped the Miracle Life," Eddie snapped. "These *must* be zombie slugs!"

"Is everything okay back there, boys?" Mr. Brewster called.

David quickly covered Eddie's mouth. "Yeah, Dad," he shouted back. "We just saw a couple of slugs, that's all."

Luckily, Mr. Brewster was so engrossed in his spike hammering, he barely looked up. "Well, there's no reason to scream, Dave," he said. "They're not going to hurt you."

"I know, Dad," David called back.

Eddie bit David's hand. "Let go of me, you jerk!" he snarled.

"Then keep your mouth shut!" David hissed back. "Listen to me. The grass might be from the Miracle Life, but the bugs are just from the dampness."

"The grass *might be* from the Miracle Life?" Eddie repeated incredulously.

"Okay," David admitted. "It *is* from the Miracle Life."

"And so are the bugs!" Eddie screamed in his face.

"They are not!" David said. "Bugs don't die under the earth, you moron. The grass must have stirred up the ground and sent the bugs running. I guarantee you the bugs are going to bury themselves again in a minute. Just watch."

Sure enough, the bugs started to burrow.

"You see?" David pointed at the ground. "There's nothing to freak out about."

"Oh, yeah?" Eddie shot back. "Well I *am* freaking out. And I'm not sure I want to sleep out anymore, either. Your dad was right. The ground is too soggy. And there are too many creepy crawlers under it."

"Oh, come on," David begged. "Don't be such a wimp. We've got plastic on the ground in our tent. There's no way the creepy crawlers can get to us."

"You better hope not," Eddie grumbled. "Otherwise, I'm packing it in."

David and Eddie approached the tent just as Mr. Brewster finished driving in the last spike.

"Now this is the perfect tent," he said, stepping back to admire his work.

"It's great, Dad." David complimented his father's efforts.

"Come inside and see how symmetrical it is," Mr. Brewster insisted.

David rolled his eyes. But he and Eddie dropped to their knees and followed Mr. Brewster through the flap.

David oohed and aahed at everything, hoping to get rid of his dad quickly. But instead of accepting the praise and heading for the house, his dad began preaching about the importance of pole placement.

David was sure the speech would never end—until a horrible hiss tore through the air.

"Darn that Dick Ellis," Mr. Brewster said angrily. "I told

him to keep that vicious cat of his out of our yard!"

Five razor-sharp claws cut through the canvas.

"That's it!" Mr. Brewster barked. "I've had it with that furball. And I've had it with Ellis too!"

"Why don't you go over there and give Mr. Ellis a piece of your mind, Dad?" David suggested.

"That's exactly what I'm going to do," Mr. Brewster said.

Yes! David thought. No way his Dad would want to finish the tent speech now. As soon as Mr. Brewster was done chewing out Mr. Ellis, he'd head into the house to tell Mrs. Brewster all about it. Then David and Eddie could finally set about disturbing the peace themselves.

Mr. Brewster pulled back the tent flap. "Where are you, you mangy beast?" he yelled.

The cat was nowhere to be seen.

"He must have run up a tree or something, Dad," David said, peering through the flap.

"When I'm done with Dick Ellis, he's going to want to run up a tree too," Mr. Brewster snarled. He headed through the yard and into the driveway.

"You want to go watch?" Eddie asked David.

David nodded. No way he was going to miss this confrontation.

But as David crawled out of the tent, he noticed something inside the Ellises' house that he wasn't expecting to see—namely, the Ellises' cat. It was curled up on the love seat in front of the big bay window.

"Uh-oh," David told Eddie. "My dad's about to ream Mr. Ellis for nothing." He pointed toward the window.

"We'd better stop him," Eddie said.

David was about to do just that when a creature far more vicious than the Ellises' cat leaped in front of him, prepared to attack.

CHAPTER

12

Raaaaaaarrrrreeeee! Hhhhissssssssss!

David's heart sank to the pit of his stomach as the mud-covered creature with black and brown fur arched its skeletal back and bared its rotting fangs.

"Holy smoke!" Eddie cried, backing away from the horrible sight. "Whose cat is that?"

David was almost afraid to answer as he stared at the muddy-white "socks" covering the cat's front paws. In his entire life, David had seen only one calico cat with white socks—his own. The problem was, he hadn't seen his cat in years.

"I hate to say this," he told Eddie, swallowing hard. "But I think she's mine."

"What do you mean, she's yours?" Eddie snapped. "You don't have a cat, you dork!"

"No." David gulped. "But I did."

"I thought you told me she died."

"She did," David told him. "Three years ago."

"Then how can this be your cat?" Eddie hissed even louder than the beast.

David shot Eddie a look that said *What are you, stupid?*

Eddie turned as white as their tent. "Don't tell me you hit the pet cemetery already?" he gasped.

"How could I have hit the pet cemetery?" David demanded. "I've been with you the whole time."

"Then this can't be your cat." Eddie heaved a sigh of relief.

"Oh, yes, she can," David insisted. "She's definitely Tabby."

At the sound of her name, the growling cat's ears perked up.

"You see?" David said. "She recognizes her name!"

"How the heck can that be Tabby?" Eddie was still confused. "You just told me you weren't in the pet cemetery."

"I wasn't," David answered. "But neither was Tabby."

This time, Eddie shot David a look.

"There wasn't enough room for her by the side of the house," David explained. "So my dad buried her under the maple tree."

"You mean the maple tree back there?" Eddie pointed to the part of the yard where David had dropped the Miracle Life.

David nodded sheepishly. "I totally forgot about it until now," he said.

Eddie's eyes looked like a couple of Ping-Pong balls about to pop out of his head.

"I told you Miracle Life would work on animals!" David exclaimed. His fear was quickly being replaced by excitement over raising the dead. "Is this too cool, or what?"

"How do we know for sure that's your cat?" Eddie asked. "She could just *look* like your cat."

"No way," David said. "Do you know how rare it is for a calico cat to have white socks?"

"It may be rare," Eddie admitted, "but it's not impossible."

"Then why is she all bony and covered with mud, as if she just clawed her way out of a grave?" David asked.

"Maybe someone abandoned her in a ditch. Or maybe she's one of those sewer cats. Did you ever think of that?"

"She's not a sewer cat! Are you, Tabby?" David said.

The cat lowered her back and started to purr.

"Check it out," David told Eddie. "I think she recognizes me." He crouched down and stuck out his hand for the cat to inspect. "Come here, Tabby," he cooed, as if he were talking to a baby. Then he kissed at the air, coaxing her.

The cat took a step forward, sniffing at David tentatively.

Eddie, however, took a step back. "You're out of your mind," he told David. "What if that thing attacks you?"

"She's not going to attack me," David continued to argue. "Tabby loves me, don't you, Tabby?"

The cat crept a little closer.

Step, sniff.

Step, sniff.

"You see?" David said. "She's coming to me."

"So?" Eddie said. "Even a stray will come if you coax it."

By then, the cat was close enough for David to touch.

"Watch," David said. "The minute I pet her head, she'll roll onto her back so I can rub her stomach. That's what she always used to do. There's no way a stray would do that, right?"

"Probably not," Eddie agreed.

"Then I'm about to prove to you once and for all that this is really Tabby," David claimed.

But as David reached up to stroke the matted fur on the cat's head, she let out a horrible screech. Then she bared her claws and took a swipe at him.

David saw the paw full of daggers and quickly pulled his hand away.

Unfortunately, he wasn't quick enough. One of the cat's claws caught David's flesh and ripped through his skin.

"Yeeeee-ouch!" David yelped as the gash on his hand began to bleed.

"I told you that was a sewer cat!" Eddie cried, backing away even farther. "I told you she was going to attack. You better hope that thing doesn't have rabies," he said, picking up a stick for protection. "Otherwise, you're going to end up camping out in the hospital!"

David winced at the thought.

"Stay back," Eddie warned the cat, swinging his stick through the air like a sword.

The cat stood her ground. But she didn't growl. And she didn't attack. In fact, she licked her chops contentedly—then rolled onto her back and started to purr.

David was stunned, but he was more convinced than ever that this was his cat. "You see," he told Eddie, nursing his wounded hand. "I told you she'd roll over so I could rub her stomach." He took another step toward the cat. But Eddie grabbed him by the back of his shirt and pulled him away.

"Are you nuts?" Eddie shrieked. "That cat doesn't want her stomach rubbed. She wants to scratch your eyes out!"

The cat meowed innocently, peering at David.

"She does not!" David defended the beast. "I probably just frightened her by moving so fast. Plus she's probably freaked out by being alive again. I mean, wouldn't you freak out if you'd been dead for three years?" He pulled away from Eddie and moved back toward the cat.

"All I know is that you're the one who's going to freak out when this sewer cat rips your eyes out!" Eddie said.

"She's not going to hurt me again," David insisted. He reached out slowly to pat the cat's stomach.

"Don't do it!" Eddie exclaimed.

But David ignored him. "It's okay, Tabby," he said, touching the cat's stomach gently. "I'm not going to hurt you."

The cat purred at David's touch. Then she lifted her head and licked his hand.

"Look," David told Eddie as the sandpaper tongue swiped his skin. "She's kissing me."

"She's not kissing you!" Eddie shouted. "She's licking your blood!"

David looked down to see the cat lapping up the tiny, red droplets on his hand.

"Oh, gross!" He tried to pull his hand away slowly so he wouldn't startle the cat. But she grabbed his hand with her paws and held it in place.

"Don't do that, Tabby," David scolded.

But the cat continued to lap up his blood with the enthusiasm of Dracula, licking harder and harder until she was practically rubbing David's skin off.

"Stop it!" David cried, jerking his hand away.

The cat sprang to her feet and quickly reared back, ready to pounce.

"Get away from her!" Eddie yelled.

David jumped back so fast, he fell on his butt.

"Get out of here, you mangy beast!" Eddie tossed his stick at the cat's head just as she was about to spring forward.

Luckily, the stick hit its mark, and the cat took off like a shot.

"What did you do that for?" David hollered. "You scared her away!"

"No duh!" Eddie screamed back. "That's what I was trying to do, you moron."

"Tabby!" David called into the darkness as he rose to his feet. "Tabby, come back!"

"Don't call that rabies-infested sewer cat!" Eddie snapped.

"It's not a rabies-infested sewer cat!" David told him. "That's my dead cat! I'll prove it to you!"

"What are you going to do?" Eddie asked. "Dig up her grave?"

"I'm going to do better than that," David promised. "I'm going to show you a dead pet digging up its own grave!" He reached through the tent flap and grabbed the bag of Miracle Life and the flashlight.

"Oh, no." Eddie started to freak. "I don't want to do this now."

"Tough," David huffed. "We're going to!"

But as David dragged Eddie toward the pet cemetery, someone else crossed their tracks. And he was way bigger and angrier than Tabby.

CHAPTER 13

"Can you believe this?" Mr. Brewster yelled as David and Eddie froze in their tracks. "That Dick Ellis told me his cat hasn't been out of the house all night. Can you imagine that? What gall this guy has. Did he really think I was going to swallow that line of manure? No way I was going to let Dicky boy get one over on me. You should have seen his face when I chewed him out twice as bad for lying to me like a worm."

David and Eddie exchanged looks. But neither one interrupted the tirade.

"Then he had the nerve to show me the cat," Mr. Brewster continued. "Like that proves he's telling the truth. 'So the cat beat me to the house,' I told him. Does this guy think I'm some kind of moron?" He paused for a moment, as if he were waiting for a response.

But David wasn't about to offer one. He was pretty sure it would be the wrong answer. David knew that when his dad went on a rip, it was best just to listen.

"One of these days," Mr. Brewster continued to rant, "those Ellises are going to push me a little too far. I tell the guy that I'm out here in my own backyard building a tent with my son and his friend when that rabid cat of his attacks us, and the man doesn't even apologize. How ignorant can one person be?"

This time, the look on Mr. Brewster's face told David he'd better say something.

"People can be real ignorant," he concurred.

"Tell me about it, Dave," Mr. Brewster grumbled. "That Dick Ellis is just lucky I didn't call the cops on him. That's what *he* would have done if we had a cat that attacked his tent. Hey," he said suddenly, "what are you guys doing down here when your tent is up there?"

"Nothing, Dad," David lied.

"Well, you must be doing something, Dave," Mr. Brewster said. "Because you both look as guilty as Dick Ellis's cat."

David couldn't believe it. How could parents always find a way to snag you, even when they were preoccupied with other things?

Still, David wasn't about to fess up.

Eddie, however, was dying to. "Tell him, David," he insisted.

"Tell me what?" Mr. Brewster demanded as David nudged Eddie hard.

"Nothing, Dad," David repeated, trying to think of something fast. "We were, just . . . uh . . ."

Mr. Brewster crinkled his forehead. "Just, uh, what?"

David's brain raced through his little white lie file, looking for an excuse that might work. "Well, if you must know, we came over here to go . . . uh . . . tinkle." He landed on a word his dad would approve of.

"You have to go tinkle?" his dad repeated.

David nodded.

"Outside?"

David nodded again. "Come on, Dad," he coaxed, weaving the little white lie into a bigger one. "Even you said that you can't go in the house to tinkle when you're camping out, because tinkling inside is for wimps."

"I said that?" Mr. Brewster asked.

"Yeah," David answered. "Last summer, when you and I camped out."

"Well," Mr. Brewster concluded, sounding just as confused as he looked, "I guess if you're going to rough it, you've got to rough it all the way."

David smiled.

"Just don't kill any of your mother's plants," he told David. "Otherwise, we'll never hear the end of it."

"Don't worry, Dad," David assured him. "We'll watch where we're going."

"You do that." Mr. Brewster headed for the sliding glass door that led into the kitchen. "If you guys need anything, I'll be inside," he said. "Just wait until your mother hears what those Evil Ellises did now."

As soon as Mr. Brewster slid the door shut behind him, Eddie started to whine.

"Why didn't you just tell your dad the truth?" he asked. "Why didn't you tell him that the Ellises' cat really was in their house the whole time and that you think Tabby attacked the tent?"

"Because we don't have any proof," David told him. "At least not about Tabby, anyway. Not since you made her run away."

Eddie rolled his eyes.

"We can tell him the truth when we bring Bullet and Dershowitz back," David said, taking another step toward the pet cemetery.

"I don't want to bring Bullet and Dershowitz back." Eddie grabbed David's arm. "This whole thing is stupid. And it's not going to work."

"Oh, yeah?" David laughed, tugging Eddie along. "Then what's the problem?"

Eddie didn't answer as they reached the edge of the cemetery.

"You're just scared because you know it *is* going to work." David opened the bag of Miracle Life and prepared to dump some on Bullet's grave.

"I'm telling you, don't do it!" Eddie yelled. He tried to grab the Miracle Life from David's hands. As he did, David turned the bag upside down. Miracle Life covered not only Bullet's grave, but every grave in the cemetery.

"Look what you did, you jerk!" David barked, trying to stop the flow of gunk escaping from the bag.

But it was too late. The ground beneath their feet was covered with Miracle Life.

And the dead were already starting to suck.

CHAPTER 14

Eddie jumped back in horror, but David watched in amazement as the soil covering his dead pets started to bubble . . .

And belch . . .

And pulsate . . .

And churn, just the way Angelica's soil had done.

"It's working!" David exclaimed, shining the flashlight at the ground. "Something cool is about to happen!"

"You know what?" Eddie gulped, backing away even farther. "You're just as sick as your sister. Raising the dead isn't cool. It's insane!"

David laughed . . .

Until the dirt above Bullet's grave parted, and two rotting turtle claws shot through the earth.

Suddenly, David began to get nervous. "It looks like Bullet is on his way up," he told Eddie.

A moment later, a sickly green box turtle clawed his way into view.

"This can't be happening," Eddie said. He took a step back as the dead turtle moved forward.

"Bullet?" David leaned cautiously over the creeping creature with the fungus-covered, cracked shell. "Is that really you?"

The turtle opened his rotting mouth. But instead of spitting out an answer, he spit out a glob of oozing black pus.

"Oh, gross!" Eddie yelled. "That's the same gunk the big bug was puking up."

David winced too. But he still wanted to stop Bullet from getting away. "Grab him," he told Eddie as the turtle crept across the lawn.

"You grab him," Eddie shot back. "No way I'm touching that thing."

But as David was about to reach out for Bullet, the soil in the cemetery opened up to reveal another dear departed pet.

"Holy Toledo!" Eddie cried. "Who the heck is that?"

"It's Fred!" David gasped, staring at the three-legged rodent clawing his way to the top of the earth.

"Fred who?"

"Fred the hamster," David clarified. "He was one of my pets a long, long time ago. I forgot all about him."

"What happened to his leg?" Eddie asked, watching the critter hobble off after Bullet.

"I don't know," David said. "Maybe the maggots chewed it off."

"Oh, man." Eddie groaned and grabbed his stomach. "That's disgusting."

So was Fred. Not only was he missing a leg, he was missing an ear, an eyeball, and dozens of patches of fur.

David wasn't about to grab *him*.

Not that he had a chance to, anyway. Just then, a forked tongue shot up from the ground and wrapped itself around David's leg.

"Aaaaaaaaggggggghhhhhhhh!" David freaked, jumping back in a panic.

The answer came a moment later when a slimy black creature suddenly surfaced.

"It's a snake!" Eddie exclaimed, staring into the beady eyes. "It's a big, ugly snake!"

"Dershowitz!" David told him. "It's Dershowitz!"

"I thought Dershowitz was the size of a garter snake," Eddie said. "Not the size of a boa constrictor!"

"The Miracle Life must have made him start growing already," David guessed. "This has to be Dershowitz. He's the only snake we ever had."

As Dershowitz slithered away, David's heart felt as if it was about to burst from his chest—just the way the pets were bursting from the ground.

"How many pets do you have down there, anyway?" Eddie asked as two big black spiders came into view.

David was wondering the very same thing. "I don't know," he told Eddie. "Maybe six or seven. I forget."

"What do you mean, you forget?" Eddie demanded as the hairy spiders crept past them.

"I mean, I forget!" David screamed. "But that's definitely Rover and Spot."

"What are they, tarantulas?"

"Yeah." David nodded nervously. "But they were tiny when they died."

"Well, they're not tiny anymore." Eddie pointed out the obvious.

Just then, a horrible buzzing sound filled the air, and a swirling black cloud rose from the earth and hovered above their heads like a humming tornado.

"It's bees!" Eddie cried out in terror. "Big, buzzing bees! Since when did you have bees for pets?"

"I didn't," David yelped, staring at the mass. "They must be from that beehive up there." He pointed to the elm tree that shaded the side of the house. "The dead ones have probably been dropping to the ground for years. That beehive's been there forever."

"Well, I think these dead bees are about to attack us!" Eddie wailed.

David was about to agree when a voice startled him into silence.

It was a voice David recognized.

And it was coming from a grave.

CHAPTER 15

"*Pretty bird . . .*"

David's heart stopped as the sound filtered through the earth.

"Who said that?" Eddie gasped, spinning around in panic.

David grabbed Eddie and spun him back toward the grave. "It wasn't Charley this time," he said, pointing down to the parting earth.

"Oh, man!" Eddie shrieked. "No way your dead pets are talking now!"

"Not *my* dead pets," David said. "It's Charley's dead pet!"

Just then, Hitch, the mynah, clawed his way out of the dirt.

Only he wasn't the size of a mynah anymore. He was the size of a raven, with the talons of an eagle.

"Pretty bird," the decomposed zombie bird with the fungus-covered beak said again. "Hitch is a pretty bird."

Not anymore, David thought.

Hitch was downright disgusting.

Aside from the squiggling maggots eating their way through his chest from the inside out, Hitch had an opening at the top of his rotting skull that was oozing black pus. And his bones were sticking straight through his featherless skin.

But the most horrifying sight of all was Hitch's glowing eyes. They weren't glowing green, the way Charley claimed his spirit droppings would. They were glowing bright red, like the eyes of pure evil.

"Get off me, you maggots," the bird screeched, plucking the bugs from his chest. "Now *you're* the dead meat," he informed them—right before he gulped down a mouthful.

David was totally grossed out and totally stunned. Charley's dead bird was talking in sentences.

"What's the matter, boys?" Hitch glared up at them. "Aren't you happy to see me? It's a miracle, after all."

David and Eddie exchanged horrified glances.

"You thought I was stupid, didn't you?" Hitch's eyes flashed with malice. "Well, you better think again." He spread his rotting wings and rose from the ground.

"Look out!" Eddie shouted as Hitch flew straight for their heads.

David ducked and covered his face.

"Come on, you guys," Hitch screeched as he whooshed

past their heads. "I'm just trying to peck your eyes out!"

David looked up in astonishment as Hitch flew through the tunnel of swarming bees and landed on a branch above them.

"What's the matter, Davey boy?" Hitch asked. "Did the cat get your tongue?"

David shook his head.

"Don't worry." Hitch laughed. "She will. Unless, of course, I get my bee buddies to swoop down and sting you to death first."

David held his breath as Hitch let out a cackle.

A moment later, the swarm started to descend, circling David and Eddie like a big, black, buzzing hula hoop.

"Help!" Eddie screamed. His body was paralyzed with fear.

David eyed the distance to the back door of the house, wondering how badly they'd get stung if they tried to break through the bee hoop and make a run for it. But the swarm was too huge and too deadly to try.

"Call them off!" David shouted to Hitch, amazed that he was pleading with a dead bird for help. "Get them away from us!"

"Say pretty please, pretty bird," Hitch ordered mockingly as one of the bees broke free from the pack and buzzed David's ear.

"Pretty please, pretty bird!" David cried.

Hitch cackled again. "Okay, guys," he called down to the bees. "Buzz off for a while."

The murdering mass immediately retreated, swirling up into the sky like a tornado.

"I wasn't really going to let them sting you to death," Hitch said as David and Eddie doubled over to catch their breath. "I was just messing with you."

"What the heck is your problem?" David asked the bird.

"Oh, I don't have a problem," Hitch replied. "But you do. *Whew-whoot!*" He whistled like a siren. "Come on up, Rex," he called. "Come here, boy!"

"Who's Rex?" Eddie demanded.

"I don't know!" David insisted.

"Don't worry," Hitch said. "I'll introduce you to him. Rex is a friend of mine from the other side. And he's been dying to meet you."

CHAPTER

16

The sound of Hitch's cackling was swallowed by the sound of the earth rumbling beneath David's and Eddie's feet.

Whatever was climbing out of the ground was bigger than the rest of the pets put together. Worse still, it wasn't rising from the cemetery.

David and Eddie jumped back in panic as two humongous paws pushed their way through the soil, right where they'd been standing.

"GRRRRRRRRRRRRRRRRRRR!" The horrible growl was followed by two snapping jaws.

"Aaaaaaaaaaaggggghhhh!" Eddie wailed as a huge dog sprang to the surface.

"Meet Rex, my buddy, my pal," Hitch said politely.

He laughed as the dog bared its dripping fangs at the

boys. "If I were you," he told David, "I wouldn't make any sudden moves."

David froze like a statue, with Eddie standing just as still beside him.

"You didn't tell me you had a dog," Eddie barked at David as the dog barked at them.

"This isn't my dog," David answered. "I don't know where he came from."

"Why don't you look at his dog tags?" Hitch dared.

Yeah, right, David thought.

"Go ahead," Hitch urged. "Stick out your hand. Rex hasn't had a decent meal in eighty years."

"That dog's been dead for eighty years?" Eddie said.

"He looks pretty good for his age, doesn't he?" Hitch responded.

"How come this dog is buried in your backyard?" Eddie asked David.

"Because we didn't always live here, you idiot," David snapped back. "This town has probably been here forever."

"Not forever," Hitch corrected. "But long enough for the dead to be countless. The living, however, are numbered."

"What the heck is that supposed to mean?" Eddie wanted to know.

"You'll see," Hitch promised. "Won't they, Rex?"

The deadly dead dog growled as it took a step forward.

David wanted to run. But he knew that if either one of them made a sudden move, the dog really would attack.

"Stay still," he told Eddie. "Otherwise, he'll rip us to pieces."

"Yes, he will," Hitch assured them.

Rex barked ferociously, then reared up as if he were about to attack.

"Run!" David cried, quickly changing his tactic.

Eddie took off like a shot, with David right behind him.

Oh, please, don't let us get eaten by a dead dog! David pleaded as he ran for his life.

As they neared the back door, David felt safe enough to turn around to see just how far from death he was.

To his surprise, Hitch and Rex weren't following at all. In fact, Hitch was perched on Rex's rotting shoulder, laughing like a loon.

"They're not following us," David told Eddie.

"Who cares?" Eddie yelped. "I'm going in the house!"

"Not without me, you're not," David said, grabbing Eddie's shirt.

"See you later, you feathered creep!" David shouted brazenly as Eddie slid open the door. Now that they were safe, David felt pretty courageous again . . .

Until Hitch shouted back.

"That's a promise," Hitch called back. "In fact, we'll *all* see you later.

CHAPTER 17

David and Eddie stayed up all night, watching out David's bedroom window for any signs of the undead.

But the backyard remained quiet and still.

Even their tent and their camping gear was left undisturbed—a fact that clearly disturbed David's dad at breakfast.

David told his father that he and Eddie hadn't slept out because the ground really had been too wet.

While his dad bought the explanation without any questions, David and Eddie had to sit through an "I told you so" lecture with their eggs.

It wouldn't have been so bad if they weren't dying to get out of the house to head back downtown to find Mortmeister.

After all, it was Mortmeister's miracle that had created their nightmare in the first place.

Finally, breakfast was over.

"Why don't you boys go outside and start taking the tent down?" Mrs. Brewster suggested.

"Actually, Mom," David said, "we need to go down to Hinkle's to get some more plant food for our science project."

"Fine," Mrs. Brewster said. "Maybe your father will agree to take down the tent."

Yes! David thought. Finally, he and Eddie could escape.

"Just be careful back there, Dad," David warned as he rose from the table.

"Be careful of what, Dave?" his father asked.

"Uh . . . the tent spikes and stuff," David said. "They're awfully sharp."

"I put them into the ground, didn't I?" Mr. Brewster said. "I'm sure I can pull them out without stabbing myself."

David smiled sheepishly. Then he turned his attention to Eddie. "You ready to go?"

Eddie's face screamed no, but he nodded yes.

"We shouldn't be long, Mom," David said as they left.

"Take your time," Mrs. Brewster called after them.

"So what are we going to tell this guy?" Eddie asked as they headed down the deserted street that led to Mortmeister's shop.

"We're going to tell him that his Miracle Life works on more than just plants," David answered.

"Like he's really going to believe us," Eddie said. "It's not like we've got a dead pet to show him."

"Look," David explained. "We've already been over this a thousand times. If anybody's going to believe us, it's Mortmeister. Besides, if he figured out a way to make Miracle Life, maybe he could figure out a way to make Miracle Death too."

"Maybe we won't need it," Eddie said. "Maybe all your dead pets ran away for good."

"You heard that bird. They're coming back to get us. And I want to be ready for them. Now just shut up and look for that blinking red sign."

"There it is," Eddie said a moment later, pointing ahead.

David followed Eddie's finger to a red sign. But it wasn't blinking. And it wasn't promising any miracles. "That's not Mortmeister's place," David said. "That's a funeral home."

"How can that be a funeral home?" Eddie asked. "We were here just yesterday, and the only store on this street was Mortmeister's."

David looked down the block, totally confused. He was sure they were on the same street. But Eddie was right. The only place open for business twenty-six hours ago was Mortmeister's shop. "I don't know," he answered. "But that sign says 'Farkas's Funeral Home.'"

"So what do you want to do?" Eddie asked nervously.

"I guess we should go down there and see," David said. "Maybe the funeral place is new. Maybe it's blocking Mortmeister's sign."

But as David and Eddie moved closer, they saw that

the only place open for business now was Farkas's Funeral Home.

"How can this be?" David wondered as they stood in front of the home for the dead.

"I don't know." Eddie cringed. "Funeral homes give me the creeps. Let's just get out of here."

"No," David protested. "Maybe somebody inside can tell us what happened to Mortmeister's store. Maybe he moved or something."

"Overnight?" Eddie asked incredulously.

"What else could have happened to him?" David snapped.

A few minutes later, David got his answer, and he didn't even have to step into the funeral parlor to do it. The doors to the funeral parlor opened, and a thin man in a black suit stepped outside.

"Can I help you, boys?" he asked, eyeing them suspiciously. "I'm Fester Farkas, undertaker and owner of this peaceful establishment."

"We were just looking for Mr. Mortmeister," David said, swallowing hard.

"Mortmeister?" the mortician repeated. "You missed that funeral by a week."

Eddie shot David a look.

"What funeral?" David gulped.

"Mr. Mortmeister's funeral," the undertaker replied.

"It's got to be a different Mortmeister," David said. "The Mortmeister we're looking for owned a plant store."

The mortician nodded. "Yes, that's right. He claimed to be some kind of botanical scientist as well."

"Right!" David blurted, sure that the misunderstanding was about to be cleared up. "He discovered this plant food called Miracle Life."

"Oh, right." The undertaker chuckled. "In fact, his will specified that he be buried with a bag full of the stuff. Apparently he believed that Miracle Life worked on more than just plants."

Eddie turned as white as the clientele inside the funeral home.

"Yes, Mr. Mortmeister is dead," the undertaker said. "Unless his discovery really worked the way he thought it would." He chuckled under his breath. "What a dope. Miracle Life. Now that's an idea for the birds."

David felt the blood draining from his body—without the help of Fester Farkas.

CHAPTER

18

"What do we do now?" David sighed as he and Eddie hurried out of the bad section of town, feeling discouraged, defeated, and totally freaked out.

Eddie didn't answer. He just shrugged hopelessly.

"We've got to get rid of the dead pets," David decided, "before they do something really horrible."

"I told you we shouldn't have brought them back to life in the first place," Eddie pointed out.

"I know," David agreed. "We should have known there was something wrong with that Mortmeister guy right from the start."

"We did," Eddie reminded him. "You were just so terrified of failing that stupid science project that you wouldn't listen to me. I knew there was a problem when Mortmeister started biting off his fingernails."

"Oh, man." David groaned. "No way we bought Miracle Life from a dead guy."

"You know what that means, don't you?" Eddie asked, stopping in his tracks. "It means we really could bring your Aunt Louise back to life."

"Don't even think that," David said as the two of them stopped in front of a shop window on one of the safer streets downtown. "It's bad enough that we've got dead pets running around. We don't need dead relatives stalking us too."

Just then, David felt a prickling sensation at the back of his neck.

"What's wrong?" Eddie asked when he saw David shudder.

"I don't know," David told him. "All of a sudden, I feel like someone's watching us."

Eddie looked up and down the street, then spun around to check behind them. He let out a scream.

David turned his head so fast, he heard his neck crack. "Aaaaaggghhhh!" David screamed right along with Eddie.

The two boys *were* being watched—by the most ferocious eyes David had ever seen.

A teenager passing by on the street laughed at them. "What weenies."

"There's nothing to be afraid of," an old woman walking behind the teen assured them.

David and Eddie looked at one another in red-faced embarrassment as they realized the woman was right.

"Those vicious-looking animals in the shop window

can't hurt you," she went on. "They're not alive. They're stuffed. This is a taxidermist's shop."

"A taxidermist's shop?" Eddie repeated.

"Yes," the woman answered. "It's a place where they stuff animals to make trophies out of them."

"Real animals?" David asked.

The woman nodded. "Well, they're dead, of course."

"Gross!" Eddie said exactly what David was thinking.

"I agree," the woman said, wrinkling her nose. "But they're nothing to be afraid of." She smiled reassuringly and gave them a little wave as she walked off.

Eddie peered through the window into the shop. "This place is even creepier than the funeral home."

"For real." David nodded. But an idea popped into his head. "Let's go inside," he said, moving toward the door.

Eddie grabbed his arm. "Are you crazy? I don't want to go in there. I'll bet whoever works there is even scarier than that Mortmeister guy. Think about it. What kind of weirdo spends all day taking the guts out of dead animals so he can stuff them and make them into trophies?"

"Maybe the kind of weirdo who can tell us how to make dead animals stay dead," David answered.

"I see your point." Eddie let go of David's arm so he could open the door.

As David stepped through the entrance into the taxidermist's shop, the hairs on the back of his neck began to prick up again. Dozens of predatory eyes glared at him from all over the store.

There were bats and owls and hawks mounted on pedestals high along the walls, all with their wings spread wide as if they were about to swoop down on unsuspecting prey.

A huge grizzly bear stood in the center of the shop. He reared up on his hind legs, clawing at the air, his mouth open in a silent roar.

A mountain lion crouched in the corner, and a smiling alligator slithered out from behind the counter.

But there were no people in the shop.

"Hello," David called out nervously.

"I'll be right with you," a voice answered.

David and Eddie followed the sound to an open door at the back of the shop. David peeked through the doorway and let out a loud gasp.

A man in a white lab coat was bent over a large metal table that looked like it belonged in a morgue. The man had a shiny scalpel in his hand and was poised to cut into a big, hairy monkey with a red and blue face and huge teeth.

The taxidermist stopped his work when he heard David gasp. He looked up at the two boys. "Well, hello there," he said in a friendly voice. "What can I do for you?"

"We'd like to ask you some questions," David replied.

"Yeah," Eddie piped up. "About dead animals."

"Well, you've come to the right place," the taxidermist said, putting down his scalpel. "I'll try to answer any questions you have. Just give me a minute to wash up.

I work with a chemical called Preserve-x. It keeps dead animals looking good as new. But it's very bad for living things." He opened the door to a small washroom. "Why don't you have a look at my latest project while I'm in here? That big baboon is called a mandrill. Interesting beast. Just don't get too close." With that, he closed the door.

"This is one scary-looking monkey," Eddie said, pushing past David to get a closer look.

"No kidding," David agreed as the two of them inched their way toward the operating table. "Imagine what would happen if we poured Miracle Life on him."

They didn't have to imagine it. All of a sudden, the big hairy monkey lying on the table began to twitch.

CHAPTER 19

"Hey, Mister! Mister!" David and Eddie screamed as the baboon continued to twitch.

"I think there's something wrong with your dead monkey," Eddie cried, backing away from the table.

"Maybe somebody really did give him a dose of Miracle Life," David suggested, backing away too. But he didn't take his eyes off the creature. He watched as the mandrill's stomach expanded, as if the animal were taking a deep breath.

"Oh, man." Eddie winced. "That thing is definitely coming back to life."

"Hey, Mister," David hollered. "You'd better get in here quick. Your dead monkey isn't so dead anymore."

The mandrill punctuated David's point by letting out a gigantic, smelly burp.

At the same time, the taxidermist came back into the

room, drying his hands. "What's all the commotion about?" he asked.

"Didn't you just hear that?" Eddie gestured toward the mandrill.

"Yes, I did," the taxidermist said, trying to hide a smile.

"Your monkey's alive!" David exclaimed.

"No," the taxidermist said, shaking his head in amusement. "I assure you, he is not."

"Oh, yes, he is," Eddie insisted. "In case you didn't know, dead monkeys don't burp."

"Actually, they do," the taxidermist informed them. "You see, when an animal dies, it starts to ferment, creating a buildup of gas in the body. The gas has to escape somehow. I'm sorry if that scared you."

"You're telling us this guy is really, truly, completely dead?" David asked, just to be sure.

"Really, truly, completely," the taxidermist assured him. To prove his point, he lifted the animal's limp arm and let it fall. "See?"

"So let me ask you a question," David said. "Have you ever had a problem with dead animals staying dead?"

The taxidermist scratched his head and looked confused. "Of course not. Once something is dead, it's dead for good."

"Not necessarily," Eddie said.

"Excuse me?" the taxidermist asked, looking at Eddie curiously.

"Nothing," David butted in. He didn't want to start talking about Miracle Life. The taxidermist would never believe them anyway. Besides, David had another idea. "When we first came in, you were talking about some chemical you use in your work."

"Preserve-x," the taxidermist told him.

"That keeps dead animals dead?" David asked.

"It preserves dead animals," the man answered.

"Good enough," David said. "Can we buy some?"

"Absolutely not," the taxidermist told him. "Preserve-x can be a very dangerous chemical in the wrong hands. Only licensed taxidermists can get it. I could go to jail if I sold it to children."

"But you don't understand—" Eddie started.

David shook his head at Eddie to cut him off. The man would never understand.

"Is there anything else I can do for you?" the taxidermist asked. "If not, I really ought to get back to work."

"I guess that's all," David conceded. "Thanks for talking to us."

"No problem," the man said, turning his attention back to the mandrill.

David and Eddie left the shop no better off than when they had entered. "Once something is dead," the taxidermist's voice echoed in David's head, "it's dead for good." *Yeah, right, buddy,* David said to himself.

"Hi, kids." An obnoxious voice interrupted David's thoughts.

David didn't have to look up to know who it was.

"Having a nice day?" Hitch asked as he swooped down in front of their faces.

David scanned the street in panic to make sure Hitch's buddies were nowhere in sight.

Luckily, the bird was the only dead animal to be seen.

"Why are you torturing us?" David asked, swatting at the hideous creature.

Hitch squawked a harsh bird laugh as he evaded David.

"Don't you remember how Charley used to love you?" David went on, trying to inspire some guilt.

"Charley." Hitch repeated her name lovingly. "Charley loves Hitch," he said in the singsong way Charley used to talk to him.

"So why doesn't Hitch love Charley and be nice?" Eddie snarled at the bird.

"Hitch does love Charley," the bird answered. "Hitch loves Charley so much that he'd like to give her a great big hug. Problem is, Hitch is a bird, and birds can't hug. So Hitch had to send someone else to hug Charley— someone who will hug Charley so tight, he'll squeeze the life right out of her."

"What are you talking about, you dirty bird?" David demanded to know.

"Dershowitz," Hitch answered. "I sent him to hug Charley for me. I bet he's giving her a nice big squeeze right now."

With that, the mangy mynah flew off, his malicious laughter echoing behind him.

"Oh, yeah," the bird squawked. "Hitch loves Charley to death."

CHAPTER 20

"We'd better go back to my house right now!" David cried, hoping they could get there before it was too late to save Charley. The two boys took off running.

"Whoa, whoa, whoa," David's mother said, blocking their path as they burst through the kitchen door. "What's the big hurry?"

"I've got to talk to Charley," David gasped, pulling himself to a stop just inches before he crashed into his mom. A cramp in his side doubled him over. "Where is she?" he asked, trying to catch his breath.

"She's upstairs, locked in her room as usual," his mother replied. "But she should be here any minute. I've just called her for lunch."

"So, she's okay?" Eddie asked breathlessly, doubled over beside David.

"Of course she is," Mrs. Brewster answered, looking at both boys curiously. "Why shouldn't she be?"

"No reason," David lied.

His mother stood there for a moment, looking as if she were trying to decide whether or not to believe him. Then she just shrugged and stepped toward the kitchen counter. "Why don't you two have some lunch too?" she said. "I made a big pot of chili, and I've got a bag of the tortilla chips you like." She reached for a chip in a bowl that sat on the counter.

David and Eddie were headed out of the room when Mrs. Brewster's scream stopped them in their tracks.

"What the heck is this?" she shrieked.

David turned and saw his mother fling a tortilla chip halfway across the room. Hanging onto the chip was a big black tarantula.

"Holy cow!" David exclaimed. "It's Spot!"

"Spot?" Mrs. Brewster said.

"David's dead tarantula!" Eddie clarified as David slowly approached the eight-legged mutant.

"At least I think it's Spot," David told her.

The tarantula ran under the refrigerator.

"Don't start this nonsense again," Mrs. Brewster said. "That can't possibly be Spot. Spot's dead."

"Not anymore," Eddie blurted.

"This is not funny," Mrs. Brewster snapped. "I don't know how you boys managed to plant that disgusting bug in that bowl of chips. I can't believe you'd go that far just to pull a practical joke on me."

"This isn't a joke, Mom," David protested. "This is for real. We've got big problems."

"No," Mrs. Brewster said. "*You've* got big problems. Your father is in the backyard, cleaning up your mess. I want you to go get him right now so he can find that spider and get rid of it."

"But, Mom, you don't understand—"

"I don't want to understand," she continued angrily. "Just go get your father. Maybe he'll understand your warped sense of humor."

David knew he had no choice but to obey. "Come on," he said to Eddie as he headed toward the door.

"You're getting to be just as difficult as your sister," Mrs. Brewster huffed.

Charley! David remembered with alarm.

She hadn't come downstairs yet. Maybe she couldn't. David knew he and Eddie had to go check on her. But first he had to get his father into the kitchen.

"Dad!" he called as he hurried out the back door into the yard. "Dad!"

His father didn't answer.

That was because he'd already finished with the tent and was sound asleep in the hammock.

"Dad!" David shouted even more urgently when he saw two more of his dead pets up to mischief.

Tabby the cat was busy positioning a garden rake—with the sharp prongs face up—directly underneath Mr. Brewster's back.

Meanwhile, Fred the hamster was gnawing on the

nylon rope that held up Mr. Brewster's hammock. He was down to the very last thread.

"Dad! Look out!" David screamed at the top of his lungs.

Mr. Brewster began to stir.

But it was too late. With one last bite, Fred cut through the rope.

"No!" David cried, watching in horror as his father crashed to the ground.

CHAPTER 21

"*Aaaaaggghhhh!*" Mr. Brewster let out a loud shout as he hit the ground.

David covered his eyes. He couldn't bear to see his father impaled on the sharp spikes of the rake.

"We'd better go get your mom," Eddie urged.

"No!" David said, lowering his hands from his eyes to grab Eddie. "I don't want my mom to see this." He mustered up the courage to take a quick glance at his father.

Mr. Brewster lay motionless on the ground.

The dead pets were nowhere to be seen.

"We've got to get help," Eddie insisted, struggling to break free of David's grip.

"It's okay," Mr. Brewster groaned, pushing himself up onto his elbows. "I'm all right. Just a little stunned by the fall."

David looked at his father more closely, relieved to find that he hadn't landed on the rake. When the hammock started to fall, his father must have rolled out of it instead of dropping straight down. He was a good two feet away from the gardening tool.

"Dad." David snapped out of his panic and ran to help his father up. "Thank goodness you're not hurt."

"Well, I wouldn't exactly say that," Mr. Brewster grumbled as he got to his feet. "I feel pretty banged up. What on earth happened to this hammock?" He moved to inspect the damage. Then he saw the rake. "How did this get here?" he asked, looking at David as if it might be his fault.

"I don't know," David lied. He was sure his father would never believe it was all part of some sinister plot cooked up by all their dear departed pets. After all, his mother had seen Spot with her own two eyes and she refused to believe it.

The thought of his mother reminded David of why they'd come outside in the first place. "Mom needs you in the kitchen," he told his father.

"Is something wrong?" he asked, hearing the urgency in David's voice.

"Yeah," Eddie chimed in. "There's a giant dead spider in there that she wants you to catch."

Mr. Brewster rolled his eyes. "If the spider's already dead, what's the problem?"

David and Eddie exchanged looks. But neither of them bothered to enlighten him.

"All I know is that Mom wants you in the kitchen right now," David said.

"All right," his father groaned. "I'll deal with this broken hammock later." With that, he limped toward the kitchen door.

"We've got to find Charley," David told Eddie as soon as his father was out of earshot.

"Right," Eddie agreed. "Let's just hope we're not too late."

David didn't even want to think about that possibility. While he wasn't particularly fond of his sister, he didn't want anything terrible to happen to her. "Let's go in the front door," he suggested. "That way we'll be able to avoid my parents."

"Good thinking," Eddie said as they ran around the house. They went in through the front door and dashed upstairs.

"Charley!" David called.

There was no answer.

"Charley," Eddie echoed as they approached her closed bedroom door.

He was answered by a muffled scream and the sounds of a struggle.

David burst through the door, prepared to do whatever it took to rescue his sister.

But when he got inside the room, there was no sign of her anywhere.

"Charley?" he called again.

"Where'd she go?" Eddie asked.

There was another muffled scream.

"It's coming from under the bed," David said.

Just then, something else came from under the bed—a slithering black tail.

"Dershowitz!" David gasped. There was something horrifyingly different about his dead pet.

Judging from the thickness of his tail, Dershowitz was growing again. In less than twenty-four hours, Dershowitz had gone from the size of a ten-foot boa constrictor to the size of a bone-crunching thirty-foot anaconda.

CHAPTER 22

"Charley!" David screamed.

"Help!" Charley's voice answered. It was weak and breathless, barely audible.

"That snake is choking the life out of her," Eddie said.

"We've got to save her," David cried.

The two boys sprang into action. They hit the floor like guerrilla warriors, then crawled under the bed where the struggle was taking place.

Dershowitz was coiled around Charley's body like a giant, murderous Slinky.

"We've got to pull him off," David said to Eddie. He tried to get his fingers between the snake's body and his sister's. But the snake had such a tight grip that it was impossible.

"This isn't going to work," Eddie decided. "We should pull them both out from under the bed first."

"Good idea," David agreed, already squirming out backward.

"Don't leave me!" Charley pleaded in a voice that was barely a whisper.

"We're not going to leave you," David assured his sister. "We're going to save you."

"You grab the snake and I'll grab Charley's feet," Eddie said to David when the two of them emerged from under the bed.

David didn't want to grab the snake. It was way too disgusting. Scaly skin was peeling off in big chunks, and it smelled like rotting sewage.

"You grab the snake," David told Eddie.

But Eddie already had a grip on Charley's feet and was tugging away. "Help me out, will you?" he grunted.

David swallowed the bile that was climbing up his throat and grabbed Dershowitz's tail. The snake slipped from his grasp with the first tug, leaving him with a handful of flaky snake skin.

David got a better grip. Then he pulled again.

This time, he and Eddie made some progress.

"Pull again," Eddie instructed.

One more good tug, and Charley and Dershowitz were out from under the bed.

"Charley, are you okay?" David asked.

He got no answer. His sister was a sickly shade of blue-gray. Her breathing had stopped.

"We're not going to be able to unwind this snake from Charley's body," Eddie said as he pushed and pulled at the monster. "We're going to have to kill him."

"How can we kill him?" David yelped. "He's already dead!"

"I've got an idea." Eddie sprang to his feet, leaving David to struggle with the snake by himself.

"What are you doing?" David hollered at his friend.

Eddie didn't bother to answer. He snatched a ballpoint pen from Charley's desk and stabbed Dershowitz with it.

"Way to go!" David exclaimed.

As Eddie withdrew his weapon to strike again, black ooze poured from the wound.

Meanwhile, Dershowitz uncoiled the top half of his body and turned to hiss angrily at the two boys.

David refused to be intimidated. "Get him again," he told Eddie.

Eddie drove the pen into the monster a second time with even greater force.

A new wound appeared—but the first wound started to heal.

"It's not going to work!" David cried, watching the snake's skin heal.

Luckily, the snake was so angry, he let go of Charley to take on the boys instead.

"Come and get me," David dared. He got to his feet and began backing toward the door, taunting the snake all the way.

Dershowitz followed, hissing angrily as he slithered along, preparing to attack.

David continued backing away, weaving from side to side, trying to fake out the snake.

As David reached the doorway, Dershowitz lunged for his throat.

That was exactly what David had hoped would happen. At the very last instant, he ducked out of harm's way and Dershowitz sprang past him into the hallway.

David slammed the door shut and threw his body against it.

"How's Charley?" he asked Eddie.

"I think she's coming around," Eddie answered. He was kneeling beside her, patting her hand and her face to try to bring her back to consciousness.

"Open the window," David suggested. "Give her some fresh air."

Eddie did as he was told.

But it turned out to be a terrible mistake.

While the fresh air did revive Charley, the open window let in a very unwelcome guest.

"Hello, Charley," Hitch squawked as Charley pulled herself up to a sitting position. "Remember me?"

"Hitch?" Charley gasped. Then her eyes rolled back into her head and she fell back onto the floor, unconscious.

"What do you want from us, you stupid bird?" David raged at the mynah as he rushed to his sister's side.

"I want you to be just like I am," Hitch answered. "I want you all dead!"

CHAPTER

23

"Now I know why I always hated you," David raged, swatting wildly as the evil mynah dive-bombed him.

"You can hate me all you want." Hitch laughed as he swooped around David's head, eluding David's flailing arms. "It doesn't matter to me. You're just dead meat. You're all dead meat!" With that, Hitch gave David a sharp peck on the top of the head, then flew out the window, his cruel laughter echoing behind him.

"That bird's got to go," Eddie snarled.

David couldn't have agreed more. There was nothing he would rather do than annihilate Hitch. But first he had to make sure Charley was okay.

"Charley," David said, kneeling down beside her.

Charley was frighteningly pale, and she didn't seem to be breathing.

"Maybe we should do CPR," Eddie suggested as he knelt on the other side of Charley's limp body.

"Do you know how?" David asked. It was one of the things they were supposed to have learned in health class.

"No," Eddie told him. "Don't you?"

"No," David answered. He hadn't paid any more attention than Eddie had.

"Well, we'd better do something," Eddie said.

"Charley," David called as he began to pat her face gently. When he got no response, he patted a little harder. "Charley! Wake up!"

Finally, Charley's eyelids fluttered.

"She's alive!" Eddie exclaimed.

"Charley?" David patted more forcefully.

Charley's eyes snapped open.

"Thank goodness you're okay," David said, heaving a sigh of relief.

"How dare you hit me, you little twerp," Charley growled.

David didn't even realize he was still patting Charley's face until she blindsided him with a powerful left hook. She knocked him right off his knees.

"He was just trying to save your miserable life, you witch," Eddie defended his friend as he backed away from Charley to avoid taking a shot himself.

"Sure he was," Charley sneered as she sat up.

"It's true," David told her, scrambling out of reach. "Don't you remember what happened?"

A look of terror came into Charley's eyes. "The snake!" she shrieked. She sprang from the floor and up onto her bed, screaming hysterically.

"It's all right." David tried to quiet her. "The snake is gone. He's not in here anymore."

But it was useless. David's voice was drowned out by Charley's incessant screeching.

"You two put that snake in here, didn't you?" Charley accused.

"We did not," Eddie said.

"Charley, you've got to listen to us," David pleaded. "That snake was Dershowitz."

"Dershowitz is dead," Charley snapped.

"Not anymore," Eddie told her. "You know that Miracle Life we bought?"

Charley just glared at him.

"Well, David dumped a bunch of it in your pet cemetery," Eddie continued. "And now all your dead pets are trying to kill us. Especially Hitch."

Charley grew pale at the mention of Hitch's name.

"It's true, Charley," David chimed in. "Miracle Life brought all the dead pets back from the grave. You just saw Hitch with your own eyes."

David was sure that if anyone would believe their story, it would be Charley. After all, this was just the kind of stuff that fascinated her.

But David was disappointed.

"No," Charley said, shaking her head. "I saw a bird who looked like Hitch."

"It *was* Hitch," David insisted. "He even said your name! You heard him."

Charley shuddered in recognition of the truth, but she shook it off quickly. "If you two think I'm going to fall for your stupid pet tricks, you're wrong," she said.

"It's not a trick," David protested. "You've got to believe us, Charley. Something terrible is going on, and we need your help to stop it."

Charley laughed. "Trust me when I tell you that you're going to need a lot more than my help to get out of this mess, because I'm telling Mommy on you." She stepped off the bed and headed for the door.

"'Mommy?'" David snorted. The only time Charley called their mother "Mommy" was when she really wanted something—like getting David grounded for life.

"Out of my way, twerp," she said, pushing past Eddie.

"Don't open that door," Eddie warned as Charley put her hand on the knob.

She hesitated. "Why not?"

"Dershowitz is in the hallway," Eddie told her.

"Right." Charley rolled her eyes. She turned the knob and threw open the door. Then she looked out into the hallway and let out a long, bloodcurdling, horror-movie scream.

David and Eddie screamed right along with her as they raced to close the door.

But before they could, Charley strolled into the hallway and started to laugh.

David peeked out the door to see that—except for Charley—the hallway was empty.

"You two little geeks are going to need some Miracle Life yourselves when I get through with you," Charley threatened. Then she proceeded to make good on her threat. "Mommy!" she screamed. "David and Eddie just played a horrible trick on me!" She winked maliciously at David as she headed down the stairs. "And they've got a big snake in the house!" she added.

"We've got to get out of here," David said to Eddie.

"What about Dershowitz?" Eddie asked.

"He's probably long gone," David replied. "Besides, Hitch is obviously the ringleader. He's the one we've got to deal with. And since nobody will help us—"

"Nobody will even believe us," Eddie interrupted.

"Right," David agreed. "We're completely on our own. We've got to find a way to stop these pet zombies, or . . ." This time David stopped himself. He didn't want to think about the consequences.

"Let's go get that dirty bird," Eddie said.

They were halfway down the stairs when they heard David's mother calling them like a maniac. Apparently Charley had convinced her that the boys were up to no good.

David turned toward Eddie and put a finger to his lips. Eddie nodded.

They took the rest of the steps as silently as they could, then dashed out the front door.

David knew it was wrong to run away. But there was no time to waste. Something had to be done about the pet zombies. And only he and Eddie could do it.

The first thing they had to do was find Hitch.

That turned out to be easier than David imagined.

"Looking for me?" a voice squawked as the two boys stepped onto the front porch. The mangy bird was perched on a low branch of the big oak tree in the front yard.

"You bet we are," Eddie said angrily.

"Yeah," David snarled. "Because you're the one who's about to become dead meat, buster!"

"Think again," Hitch replied. Then the mynah mimicked Mortmeister's unearthly voice. "For the dead, there is life. And for the living, only death."

David's heart sank to the pit of his stomach as the bird started to laugh.

"In twenty-four hours," the menacing mynah warned in his own creepy voice, "this whole town will be zombified!"

CHAPTER 24

"**G**et back here, you flying rat!" David hollered as Hitch hopped off his perch and flew away.

"Follow that bird," Eddie said, taking off after Hitch.

David was right behind him.

They ran for what seemed like a mile.

"Uh-oh," Eddie panted finally. "It looks like Hitch is headed for the park."

"You've got that right," Hitch squawked. Then he disappeared into the trees that surrounded the playground.

"Where'd he go?" Eddie asked.

"I don't know," David said. He ran on, looking all around for the miserable mynah.

But instead of Hitch, David spotted something else.

Eddie saw it too. "What on earth is that?" he cried.

A huge black cloud rolled across the clear blue sky. But it was way too low to be a cloud—and it was buzzing.

"It's the dead bees!" David realized. "And they're heading straight for the kids on the playground!"

David and Eddie watched helplessly as the cloud suddenly burst and hundreds of bees rained down on the children and their parents.

Panic broke out immediately. The adults snatched up screaming children and ran in different directions as the bees dive-bombed them.

David and Eddie kept their distance. There was nothing they could do to help.

The nasty creatures stung everyone in sight. Their victims howled in pain as they scrambled to escape.

As the playground cleared, the bees abandoned their attack, reformed their cloud, and buzzed away.

"This is getting way out of control," David said as his heart finally started beating again.

"Tell me about it," Eddie agreed.

Suddenly, leaves rustled overhead.

David looked up just in time to see Hitch take flight.

Once again, the boys followed the bird. And once again, Hitch seemed to be leading them somewhere.

They went through the playground, over the hill, and down toward the lake where the picnic area was.

The area was deserted except for a teenage girl sitting on a blanket on the grass. She was tossing a big, multi-colored ball to a little girl who had barely learned to walk.

"Pretty baby," Hitch said, circling back so the boys could hear him.

"You leave that baby alone!" David shouted, terrified of what the zombie bird might do to the child.

"I don't think it's Hitch we have to worry about," Eddie said. "Look!" He pointed toward the high grass near the teenager and the baby.

David saw the grass move ever so slightly. "It's Tabby!" he gasped, staring at the calico cat with the white socks.

The cat was low to the ground. Her ears were back. She was ready to spring.

"Look out!" David screamed to the teenager. "That cat is about to attack the baby!"

But David's warning came too late.

CHAPTER 25

"*Nooooooooo!*" David and Eddie wailed as the cat pounced on the baby.

The two of them lunged for the animal, but the teenager jumped to her feet and blocked their path. "What do you think you're doing?" she snarled at them. "You stay away from my baby sister!"

"We're only trying to save her life," David cried, moving unsuccessfully to get past her.

"Yeah," Eddie chimed in. "That cat is very dangerous."

The teenager frowned. "Are you crazy or just stupid?" she asked.

"We're dead serious," David said as he watched the baby and the cat roll around on the grass just a few feet away.

The baby was giggling happily, as if it were all a game.

But David knew the game would turn deadly.

"You see," he started to explain hurriedly, "that's my cat. And she's been acting really strange lately because she's been . . . uh . . . sick." He decided to leave out the dead part. "In fact, she's vicious. I don't want her to hurt the baby. So if you'll just let me chase her away, everything will be fine."

"You leave that cat alone," the teenager said.

"Are *you* stupid?" Eddie threw her own words back in her face. "Why would you let your baby sister play with a vicious animal?"

"Because she's not a vicious animal," the teenager insisted. "And she's not yours either. That cat belongs to me."

"Are you sure?" Eddie asked.

"Of course I'm sure," the girl snapped. "Unlike you, I know my own cat. She's the only calico on earth with white socks. And you see that little tag dangling from her rhinestone collar? It says 'Princess.' That's her name."

David saw the collar sparkling in the sunlight. That was enough to convince him he'd been mistaken. "I guess that isn't my cat after all," he said as relief flooded his body. "I'm sorry we bothered you. We were just worried about the baby."

"It's okay," the teenager assured them, becoming a little more friendly. "Is your cat really that mean?"

A terrible caterwauling answered her question.

"There's your cat!" Eddie cried, pointing across the open field.

Tabby really was in the park. But she was busy stalking a squirrel.

"That's your cat?" the teenager gasped, watching in horror as the dead calico chased the live squirrel up a tree.

"I'm afraid so," David answered.

"That cat is really vicious," Eddie added. "If I were you, I'd scoop up your cat and your sister and get out of this park."

"Meanwhile, we'd better do something about Tabby," David said.

The two boys took off running as the teenager followed Eddie's advice.

As the boys approached the tree, David lost sight of Tabby in the thick leaves. But he could still hear the cat yowling. He was sure she was still after the squirrel, because he could see the branches shaking violently as the two animals climbed higher and higher.

"What are we going to do?" Eddie asked David as the two of them stood at the base of the tree.

David shrugged hopelessly as he caught sight of Tabby chasing the poor squirrel around and around. He didn't want to see what would happen if Tabby actually caught her prey. "We've got to stop that cat," he said, picking up some stones to throw.

Eddie followed David's lead, pitching pebbles at the ferocious beast as it raced around the tree.

But it was a hopeless cause. Even their best shots didn't come anywhere near the cat. It was way too fast, and too high in the branches. David was sure the poor squirrel was a goner. Nonetheless, the boys kept up their efforts to save its life.

But while they were busy trying to save the squirrel, they didn't notice that they were being stalked.

A deep snarl tore David's attention away from the rescue attempt. He spun around and found himself staring into the jaws of death.

For one brief moment, both David and Eddie stood frozen in terror as their ferocious attacker licked his chops hungrily.

"It's Rex!" Eddie shrieked.

Rex snarled again and curled his lips in a bloodthirsty smile. He hunkered down, looking back and forth between the two boys as if deciding which to eat first.

"Quick," David screamed at Eddie. "Climb the tree!"

Rex rushed forward, snapping at David's heels as he scrambled up onto the lowest branch.

The wild dog jumped up and down at the base of the tree, barking incessantly as the boys climbed higher.

"Help!" they called at the top of their lungs. "Somebody help us!"

But there wasn't a single person to be seen.

The only attention they drew came from Tabby. She stopped chasing the squirrel and began to climb down the tree instead.

Now the boys were trapped between the two deadly, dead beasts. Both had their teeth bared. Both intended to do serious damage.

"We're done for!" Eddie cried.

David didn't bother to protest. Eddie was right. If they climbed down from the tree, Rex would eat them alive. If they stayed where they were, Tabby was sure to rip them to shreds with her razor-sharp claws.

The cat was only inches away from them now, looking like a hideous Halloween creature. Her back was up. Her mangy fur stood on end. Her yellow, slitted eyes were wild.

But before the cat pounced, another, more horrible creature arrived on the scene.

CHAPTER
26

A maniacal screech cut through the air as Hitch dived through the tree branches toward the boys.

David closed his eyes tight, figuring that Hitch meant to peck them to death. But the bird never came near him. After a few moments, David opened one eye to find out what was going on.

He saw Hitch perched on a branch near the cat.

"Having fun?" the bird squawked. "We are," he added with a mocking laugh.

"What's the matter with you dead pets?" Eddie snapped. "Why don't you just leave us alone?"

"Because miracles don't last forever," Hitch answered. "From now on, we need flesh and blood to stay zombified."

Rex barked loudly as Tabby let out a hiss. But they weren't interested in David and Eddie. They seemed to be talking to Hitch.

"Not yet," Hitch squawked back at them.

Rex barked more insistently.

"I said no!" Hitch hollered at the dog. Then he turned his attention back to the boys. "Rex and Tabby are quite perturbed with me," he explained. "You see, they want to tear you to shreds right this second, but I won't let them."

"Why not?" David asked.

"Because this is not the time or the place," Hitch replied. "The bees messed everything up. They created such a panic, park rangers and pest control people will be here any minute. And I can't afford to attract unwanted attention before I've had a chance to reanimate our big brothers."

"Big brothers?" Eddie said.

"Reanimate?" David repeated.

Rex barked inquisitively, and Tabby meowed.

Hitch ignored the boys and answered his friends' questions instead. "We're going to need backup," he said. "So we'll bring them to life tonight after dark, when no one's downtown. Until then, lie low and try not to be seen. Now get out of here," he ordered the beasts.

Rex turned tail and ran. Tabby raced down the tree without even glancing at David and Eddie and hurried off in a different direction.

"Later, boys," Hitch screeched. Then he spread his wings and took flight, leaving David and Eddie to figure out just what kind of backup Hitch was talking about.

CHAPTER 27

David had the horrible feeling he knew exactly what Hitch was planning to do. When he and Eddie got back to the house, the bag of Miracle Life was missing.

"That dirty bird!" David ranted. "He's planning to go down to the taxidermist's shop! I just know it."

"Why would he do that?" Eddie asked. "Hitch said the dead in this town were countless. Why doesn't he just sprinkle the Miracle Life in other people's backyards?"

"Maybe he doesn't know who's buried where," David said. "Besides, you heard him. He said he wanted to wait until dark when no one was downtown."

"Uh-oh." Eddie gulped. "What if he's planning to head for Farkas's Funeral Home instead of the taxidermist's shop?"

"Nah," David said. "He's a bird. His big brothers have to

be other animals, don't you think?"

"How the heck should I know?"

"I'm telling you," David insisted, "he's going to hit the taxidermist's shop. It's the only thing that makes sense. Where else is he going to find the biggest, meanest, scariest animals on earth, all in one place?"

"You're probably right," Eddie finally agreed.

"We can't let that happen," David said. "We have to go down there tonight and stop them."

"No way!" Eddie shook his head adamantly. "I'm not going downtown after dark. We're liable to get attacked by something worse than dead animals."

"If we don't go down there and stop that evil bird, *every* part of town is going to be dangerous."

Eddie didn't protest. He couldn't.

"We started this," David went on. "Now it's up to us to find a way to end it—before everyone in town winds up being food for the dead."

CHAPTER

28

The rest of the day passed in an anxious blur as David and Eddie tried to come up with a plan to battle Hitch and his pet zombies.

They told David's parents they were working on the finishing touches of their science project, so everybody left them alone. Mrs. Brewster even let them bring their dinner up to David's room.

Neither one of the boys touched a bite. They emptied their plates into the trash can and brought the dishes back to the kitchen, telling David's mother the meal was delicious. Then they went back upstairs and locked themselves in again, waiting until darkness fell to sneak out of the house.

Sneaking out was the easiest part of the plan. The side window in David's room was right over the garage roof.

All they had to do was climb out the window, crawl to the edge of the roof, and jump to the ground.

The rest of the plan was much more complicated.

After debating the issue all afternoon, David and Eddie decided there was only one weapon they could use to battle the pet zombies. And that weapon was inside the taxidermist's shop.

"This is never going to work," Eddie said nervously as the two boys cowered outside the store.

"It's got to," David insisted. "It's our only hope." He peered through the dark windows to make sure the coast was clear. "It looks pretty quiet in there," he finally told Eddie.

"How are we supposed to get in?" Eddie asked.

"We'll have to kick open the door or smash in a window," David decided.

"Are you nuts?" Eddie gulped. "What if an alarm goes off?"

"Then the cops will come and arrest us, I guess," David said. "But what choice do we have?"

Eddie sighed. "I'm too young to go to prison."

"Would you rather be dead?" David asked.

Eddie shook his head.

"Then shut up and help me kick this door in."

"Why don't you try the knob first?" Eddie suggested.

"Yeah, right," David said. "Like it's really going to open." But he reached out anyway.

To David's surprise, the door handle turned. "Check it out!" he told Eddie. "The stupid door is unlocked!" David was so relieved, he didn't even question *why* the door was unlocked.

He should have. Because someone was waiting for them inside the shop.

"Hello, boys!" Hitch's voice assaulted them the moment they stepped through the door. "My friends and I have been waiting for you."

The lights in the shop snapped on. "It's an ambush!" Eddie cried as every dead pet in the shop suddenly reanimated.

The bats mounted on the wall swooped down, as did the owls and the hawks.

The huge grizzly bear stepped off its stand and growled murderously at the boys. The mountain lion crouching in the corner sprang forward.

"Say hello to my big brothers," Hitch squealed as he hovered above them with the bag of Miracle Life hooked over his beak.

"Get the Preserve-x!" David screamed as Eddie dove behind the front counter.

A moment later, Eddie raced back out again, empty-handed. The snapping jaws of the alligator were trying to grab hold of his butt.

"Help!" Eddie wailed. "It's a jungle back there!"

"It's a jungle out here too!" David cried, trying to avoid the swiping claws of the grizzly. "Is the Preserve-x back there?"

"I don't know," Eddie said. "The only thing I saw was him!" He pointed to the alligator chasing him around the shop.

"If I were you," Hitch cackled from above, "the only preserving I'd worry about is my own butt!"

"Drop dead, you zombie bird!" David shouted back. Then he darted through the bats and ran for the back room, where the taxidermist had been working on the mandrill.

Hitch followed, with Rex and Tabby on his tail.

Oh, please, let me find some Preserve-x, David begged as he scanned the operating table. The mandrill was still lying there, waiting to be stuffed.

He spotted a bottle right beside the body.

Yes! David thought, grabbing the bottle. "Take that, you dirty bird!" he yelled. But before he could toss some Preserve-x into the air, Hitch dropped some Miracle Life on the mandrill.

A split second later, the mandrill did more than pass gas.

"Rrrrrrrrrraaaaaaaaaaaarrrrrre!" The big baboon sprang from the table, ready to attack David.

"Aaaaaaaggggggggghhhhh!" David shrieked, splashing the Preserve-x on the big ape.

The moment the Preserve-x hit the mandrill, he froze in his place.

"It works!" David called out to Eddie. "The Preserve-x works!" He splashed some on Rex and Tabby as Eddie screamed back in panic.

"Well, get it working out here!" he cried. "This bear's about to take my head off!"

David raced toward his buddy, with Hitch overhead.

"Holy cow!" David exclaimed when he saw Eddie's head in the dead bear's mouth. Eddie struggled to hold open the jaws of death with just his hands.

"It's not a holy cow!" Eddie said. "It's a bear! Now hurry up and re-kill this sucker, will you?"

David splashed some Preserve-x on the bear's butt.

Immediately, the grizzly stopped moving, and its jaws locked in place.

"Two seconds more and I would have been dead!" Eddie gasped as he pulled his head from the beast's jaws.

"Yeah, well, don't worry about it," David said. "We're going to kill all these suckers with this stuff." He squirted the Preserve-x in every direction, killing one dead beast after another, including Dershowitz and Fred, and Rover and Spot.

"Way to go!" Eddie crowed as the dead animals died again.

"Now it's your turn," David told Hitch as he hovered over them, looking more like a chicken than a mynah.

Hitch dropped the bag of Miracle Life to the floor in panic as he tried to escape.

Luckily, he flew straight toward a closed window. Instead of smashing right through it, he slammed into the glass and knocked himself out.

"See you later, sucker," David gloated as he poured the Preserve-x onto the bird's body.

A moment later, David had the miracle he was hoping for.

CHAPTER 29

A hundred pairs of eyes stared at David and Eddie. But none of the creatures inside the taxidermist's shop moved.

"Are they all really dead?" Eddie asked, glancing around nervously.

"Yes," David assured him. "The nightmare is really over."

"Let me tell you something, pal," Eddie said. "I'm never letting you talk me into another one of your crazy schemes ever again. Miracle Life was almost the death of us."

David knew that was the truth. But he wasn't about to admit it to Eddie. "At least it wasn't a total waste," he defended himself.

"How do you figure that?" Eddie shot back.

"Miracle Life may have been a big problem with the animals," David explained, "but it worked wonders on our dead plants."

"True," Eddie admitted.

"We're going to have the best science project in the class," David said proudly.

"Won't Mrs. Wolfe be surprised?" Eddie laughed. "She's going to have to give us an A-plus."

"Our first A ever," David pointed out. "It wasn't that bad, after all."

Eddie looked around at all the vicious animals who'd tried to eat them. "Yes, it was," he told David. Then he headed for the door. "Let's get out of here."

Outside, the street was dark and deserted. It was almost as terrifying as the shop had been.

"I hate this part of town," Eddie moaned.

David didn't like it either. "Just walk fast," he told his friend, giving him a push to move him along. "We'll be home before you know it."

But as the two boys neared the first corner, a figure stepped out of the shadows, blocking their path.

"Run!" David said, grabbing Eddie to drag him in the opposite direction.

"No need to be afraid," a familiar voice called after them.

"Who are you?" David asked, glancing over his shoulder.

"Frederick von Mortmeister," the answer came.

"*Aaaaagggggggghhhhhh!*" Eddie wailed. "It's the dead

Miracle Life guy!" He tried to run, but David grabbed his arm to stop him.

"Hey, you freak," David snapped. "Why didn't you tell us that Miracle Life worked on more than plants?"

"Because that wouldn't have been any fun," Mortmeister replied.

"You're sick," Eddie shouted.

"No." Mortmeister laughed. "I'm worse than sick, remember? I'm dead." He took a step forward.

"Stay away from us, you creep!" David barked.

"Oh, but I'm hungry," Mortmeister informed them. "And you're the only food on the street."

"Let's get out of here!" Eddie cried.

But before the boys could make a run for it, the ground beneath their feet started to shake as if an earthquake were coming.

"What's going on?" Eddie yelped, grabbing David to steady himself.

The windows of the taxidermist's shop exploded as the walls began to vibrate.

"Oh, no!" David gasped. He remembered that when the bag of Miracle Life had fallen onto the floor of the shop, the mixture had spilled down between the floorboards. "I think something under that taxidermist's shop is coming to life!"

Mortmeister began to laugh. "That could be a serious problem for you boys."

"Why?" David wanted to know. "What's underneath that building?"

"It's not just under *that* building," Mortmeister explained. "In fact, this whole part of town used to be a potter's field."

"What's a potter's field?" Eddie asked.

Mortmeister laughed even harder. But he didn't answer right away. He let a few moments pass, allowing the tension to build. Then he let the boys in on his terrible secret. "A potter's field is a graveyard. Most of the people you're about to meet haven't eaten in hundreds of years."

David sucked in what he was sure was his very last breath.

Mortmeister gave an evil cackle. "Welcome to Zombieville," he said.

Get ready for more . . .

*Here's a preview of the next spine-chilling book
from A. G. Cascone*

FAERIE TALE

The first time Colin saw the Tooth Fairy was after he lost his first baby tooth. Nobody believed him, but he kept seeing her every time a tooth came out. He kind of liked it and felt pretty special. But now, Colin is starting to see other creatures in his room at night. And these fairies aren't so friendly; in fact, they're downright scary.

Colin McKay lifted his head from the pillow and slowly sat up in bed. He thought he heard something. Something more than just a bump in the night.

He heard it again—a faint, eerie humming sound.

Colin's body stiffened in fear. He squinted and searched the dark room. Then he craned his neck and peered up to the top bunk, but he couldn't see anything in the blackness except the lump in the bed above him—the lump that was his twin brother, Quint.

Colin kept perfectly still, perfectly silent for a moment. Now all he could hear was his brother's deep, steady breathing. He sighed and plopped his head back down on his pillow.

Even though he was eleven years old, the dark night still frightened Colin sometimes—a fact that amused Quint endlessly. Quint wasn't afraid of anything. He insisted the only reason Colin was afraid of the dark was because Colin read too many horror books.

Colin tried his best to ease back into sleep. He had probably imagined the noise. He yawned and touched the side of his mouth. He had a loose tooth, and the pain wasn't making it any easier to fall asleep. Unfortunately, the tooth wasn't loose enough for Colin to tie a string around it, pull it out, and put himself out of his misery.

Colin squeezed his eyes shut and thought of things that might help him fall asleep. Math class. Homework. His dad's opera CDs. That would do it. He listened to his brother's rhythmic breathing and finally felt himself drifting back to sleep. Soon his own breathing became regular and heavy.

But what had seemed like a duet suddenly sounded like a symphony to Colin. He thought he heard *more* breathing. Not his own. Not Quint's.

Colin held his breath and listened. In between Quint's puffs and snorts, he heard a strange wheezing. Colin let his breath out, then gasped.

Someone else was in the room!

Should he wake up Quint?

Calm down, Colin told himself. He closed his eyes again. His toothache had kept him awake, and now he was overly tired. His brain was probably playing tricks on him.

Besides, Quint would kill Colin if he woke him up. There had been too many false alarms in the past. There was the time Colin thought there was a gremlin in the closet, and the time he thought he saw a UFO hovering outside the window. There were even times, when he was much younger, when he was convinced he saw Santa Claus, the Easter Bunny, or the Tooth Fairy. Too many times to remember.

Quint's teasing had been unending. Recalling those times, Colin decided to ignore his fears and count sheep instead. One . . . two . . . three . . . four . . .

Suddenly he felt his mouth open. His loose tooth throbbed in pain. The wheezing was right in his face. Someone's stale breath filled his nostrils. Someone was there, watching him as he slept.

Colin snapped his eyes open. He tried to yell, but no sound escaped his mouth. Fear strangled the scream in his throat.

An ugly, winged creature stood on Colin's chest. It had pried Colin's mouth open and was peering into it. It held a miniature pair of pliers in its minuscule hands. Colin watched it as it yanked on his tooth.

The creature looked like a wart-covered, pointy-eared elfin boy. Its yellow eyes stared challengingly into Colin's, almost daring him to scream. It released a high-pitched chuckle as it went about its work. Its wings beat in the air as it pulled harder and harder on Colin's tooth.

Colin shook his head and blinked his eyes, hoping to send the vision away.

"Be still!" an impatient little voice squeaked at Colin. Rank breath wafted into Colin's face.

Colin heard the voice, loud and clear. His brain was not playing tricks on him. This was definitely not a nightmare. What was happening to Colin was real!

"Aaaaaaaaaaaaaaaaah!" Colin screamed.

About the Author

A. G. Cascone is the pseudonym of two authors who happen to be sisters . . . "The Twisted Sisters." In addition to *Deadtime Stories*, they have written six books, two horror-movie screenplays, and several pop songs, including one top-ten hit.

If you want to find out more about DEADTIME STORIES or A. G. Cascone, look on the World Wide Web at: http://www.bookwire.com/titles/deadtime/

Also, we'd love to hear from you! You can write to:
  A. G. Cascone
  c/o Troll
  100 Corporate Drive
  Mahwah, NJ 07430

Or you can send e-mail directly to:
agcascone@bookwire.com

Read all of the silly, spooky, cool, and creepy

_____	0-8167-4135-2	**Terror in Tiny Town**
_____	0-8167-4136-0	**Invasion of the Appleheads**
_____	0-8167-4137-9	**Along Came a Spider**
_____	0-8167-4138-7	**Ghost Knight**
_____	0-8167-4139-5	**Revenge of the Goblins**
_____	0-8167-4193-X	**Little Magic Shop of Horrors**
_____	0-8167-4216-2	**It Came from the Deep**
_____	0-8167-4194-8	**Grave Secrets**
_____	0-8167-4260-X	**Mirror, Mirror**
_____	0-8167-4261-8	**Grandpa's Monster Movies**
_____	0-8167-4292-8	**Nightmare on Planet X**
_____	0-8167-4293-6	**Welcome to the Terror-Go-Round**
_____	0-8167-4294-4	**The Beast of Baskerville**
_____	0-8167-4395-9	**Trapped in Tiny Town**
_____	0-8167-4396-7	**Cyber Scare**
_____	0-8167-4397-5	**Night of the Pet Zombies**
_____	0-8167-4398-3	**Faerie Tale**

$3.50 each

Available at your favorite bookstore . . .
or use this form to order by mail.

Please send me the books I have checked above. I am enclosing $_____
(please add $2.00 for shipping and handling). Send check or money order
payable to Troll Communications — no cash or C.O.D.s, please — to Troll
Communications, Customer Service, 2 Lethbridge Plaza, Mahwah, NJ 07430.

Name _____

Address_____

City _____State_____ZIP _____

Age _____ Where did you buy this book? _____

Please allow approximately four weeks for delivery. Offer good in the U.S. only. Sorry,
mail orders are not available to residents of Canada. Price subject to change.